Ansley's Big Bake Off

faithgirlz

Ansley's Big Bake Off

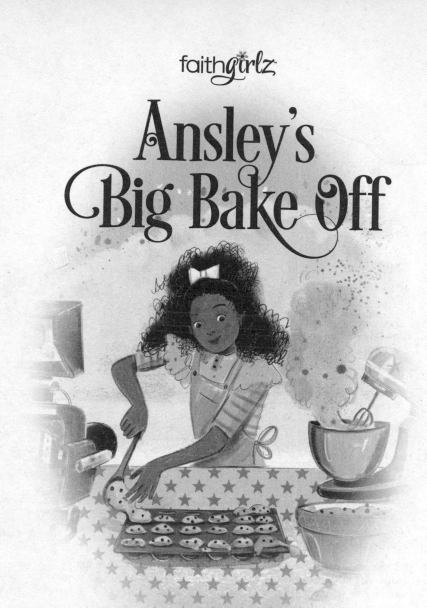

Kaitlyn, Camryn & Olivia Pitts

with Janel Rodriguez Ferrer

ZONDERKIDZ

Ansley's Big Bake Off
Copyright © 2020 For Girls Like You, Inc.
Illustrations © 2020 by Lucy Truman

Requests for information should be addressed to:
Zonderkidz, *3900 Sparks Dr. SE, Grand Rapids, Michigan 49546*

Library of Congress Cataloging-in-Publication Data
ISBN 978-0-310-76960-6

Art direction: Cindy Davis
Interior design: Denise Froehlich

Printed in the United States of America

20 21 22 23 24 LSC 10 9 8 7 6 5 4 3 2 1

From Kaity:

*To my mommy for being my biggest support.
And to my sisters for always being there for
me and for being my best friends.*

From For Girls Like You:

*To Roberta for being a gift to our
ministry that keeps giving.*

*To Janel for catching the vision and so
creatively capturing our story.*

*To our team for filling in the gaps and
holes and being God's wind in our
sails in our greatest time of need.*

Chapter 1

"Great job, Ansley." My big sister, Lena, crossed her arms and took a long, sweeping look over my room. She smiled at my soft, pink, unicorn-patterned bedspread, at the two unicorn stuffed toys lying on top of it, and at the beautiful unicorn poster hanging on the blush-colored wall over my desk. She nodded slowly. "I'm sensing a theme . . ."

I giggled. "Yup! The theme is: Ansley!" I explained. "Because Ansley equals unicorns!"

Lena pointed to the sparkly unicorn T-shirt I was wearing. "You don't say." I laughed at that. Then Lena motioned for me to follow her. "Wanna see mine now?"

"Sure!" I trotted after her.

Lena and I were putting the finishing touches on our new bedrooms in our new house. We had moved in just a few days ago, but finding the perfect place for everything was taking longer than we had expected. It had also been more fun than we thought it would be.

"Ta-da!" Lena spread out her hands and led me inside her bedroom. Her bedspread, pillowcases, and headboard were all a creamy white, making her bed look like a fluffy cloud in the middle of her room. Her curtains were a pale blue and covered with a star pattern. On one wall was an autographed poster from the movie *Above the Waters*, a movie she had actually *been* in a few years back with the famous singer Mallory Winston. And on the opposite wall hung an acoustic guitar that somehow looked as if it was just waiting for Lena to snatch it up and start strumming.

I stroked my chin, pretending to be deep in thought. "Yes . . . yes . . . this room . . . it seems to be saying something. Hmmm. What is it? I hear it! It's saying, 'Leeeee . . .' What's that now? 'Leeeeeen?' Oh, yes, that's right! *Leeeeeeena!*'" I yelled out. I lifted my arms and twirled in a circle on the rug at the foot of her bed.

Lena chuckled that time, and it made my heart do a little dance. I was glad that I had helped to cheer her up. Lena hadn't been smiling or laughing much lately—in fact, neither had my dad, my other sisters, or me, even. And I was probably the smiliest one in the family.

Because even though we were enjoying our new house and were smiling and laughing right now, we were all still sad inside. We were missing Mom. She had died unexpectedly a few weeks ago. I hadn't known until that day that surprises could be sad—even awful sometimes. Mom had been looking forward to moving into the new house as much as the rest of us. "It'll be a new adventure for the Daniels family!" she had said, smiling. And it was. Only now it was an adventure missing one very important person.

I sank down onto Lena's bed. "Everything would be just perfect if only Mom were here."

Lena sat down next to me and draped an arm over my shoulders. "Yeah." She sighed.

"But now everything's changed," I went on. "New house, new church . . . and the first day of school sure will be different too."

"Well, yeah. New school, new classmates—and no after-school snack surprise." Lena nodded.

Mom used to have a first-day-of-school tradition where she baked us an extra-special snack for when we came home. (It was different every year, and usually a sweet treat she wouldn't ordinarily let us have before dinner, like brownies or cupcakes.) Then she'd let us stuff our faces as she listened to us all tell her about how our day had gone. That was the best part, really. Mom would cup her chin in her hands and look straight into our faces as we talked. She always seemed really interested in what we had to say. She was such a great mom. And this year, with me starting middle school—in a *new* school where I didn't know *anybody* (just thinking about it made my stomach flip over like a flapjack)—I felt like I could have really used her special, loving support more than ever.

All four of us Daniels sisters were going to start school at Roland Lake Christian Academy on Monday. It was a beautiful campus with an outdoor fountain and sprawling green lawns. There was only one problem with it. The school itself was divided into three sections. The main building was over one hundred years old (it had originally been a mansion) and stood at the center. The other two buildings stuck out on either side of it, like wings. Actually, they *were* called wings—the grammar school wing and the high school wing. The middle school was, well, in the middle.

"If I was still in elementary school," I said, "I would at least be near the twins." (The twins were our sisters, Ashton, who we called "Cammie," and Amber, who we called "Kitty." More on that later.) They were nine years old. "Or if only I was already in high school, I could be in the same building as you," I told Lena. "But we're all going to be separated! I'm going to be all alone!"

Lena cocked her head. "For the first five minutes, maybe. But you'll make friends fast. You're good at that. Besides, remember what we promised each other when we moved here?"

At that moment, Cammie and Kitty popped in to check out how Lena had decorated her room.

I widened my eyes. "Great timing, you guys!"

"What?" Cammie looked a little suspicious, but Kitty had a dreamy look on her face as she admired the room.

I explained, "Lena was just about to say it." I thrust out my arm and into the middle of the circle of sisters. "You know. *It*. Remember . . . ?"

Lena placed her hand on top of mine and began, "Even in times when we're apart . . ."

"The Daniels sisters," I said, "promise with all our hearts . . ."

Cammie snapped to attention and slapped her hand on top of Lena's. Kitty immediately put hers on top of her twin's. Then they said at the same time, "That we'll always be . . ."

And suddenly it was all of us, "Together *four*-ever! Together *four*-ever! Together *four*-ever! Together *four*-ever!" (We had to say that last part four times.)

"Woooooooo!" we cheered ourselves, broke our hands apart, and beamed at one another.

"Girls!"

Our dad's voice broke the spell, and all four of us turned our heads toward the open doorway.

"Lena! Ansley! Cammie! Kitty!"

He had called us all by name. It sounded important. We all tried to bolt out of the room at the same time, unsure of even where to turn next. We still were not used to the layout of the new house.

"Um, where are you, Dad?" I called out with a nervous giggle.

"I'm in the dining room!" His voice floated back.

Wanting to make Lena smile again, I shot ahead of her and grinned playfully over my shoulder. "Beat ya there!" But before I took a step, Cammie and Kitty dashed out in front of me. They squeaked in alarm when I almost slammed into them, then squealed with delight when they peeled on ahead and thundered down the stairs. As I stared open-mouthed after them, Lena doubled over laughing at my frozen look of surprise. Then I laughed too. I may have lost the race, but getting Lena to laugh had definitely been a win.

"No running down the stairs!" Dad called out.

Once we reached the dining room, we found Dad (and Kitty and Cammie who were cheering themselves for their victory) at the dining room table. They were each standing behind the chairs they regularly sat in. When Lena and I took our places behind the chairs on Dad's right side, I noticed something. Set out in front of each of us girls—like some sort of strange placemat—was a flat, rectangular package neatly wrapped in brown paper so smooth it looked almost as if it had been ironed.

"I got these from the framer's today," Dad said, smiling around at all of us. "They're housewarming presents—one for each of you. See? Your names are on them. Go ahead and open them up. I was thinking you could hang them over your beds. Or you can choose a spot in your room that you might like better."

Since the packages were only very lightly taped closed, they fell open easily. My picture was facedown, so I couldn't see what it was until I turned it over. Once I did, I let out a small gasp.

Framed in gold was a Scripture verse in my mother's handwriting. It read: "The joy of the LORD is your strength."—Nehemiah 8:10 (NIV).

I blinked back the tears I felt forming in my eyes and quickly looked around the table at my sisters. They were all admiring their own different Scripture verses—also written in Mom's handwriting.

Lena found her voice first and asked for all of us, "How . . . ?"

Dad turned toward the laptop bag he had propped on his chair, reached into it, and pulled out a very familiar-looking, slightly messy notebook stuffed with folded sheets of paper and brightly colored sticky notes. It was one of Mom's prayer journals. "As you girls know, your mom read the Bible every day. And when she did, she often wrote down the Scripture she was praying over or verses she felt inspired by. When I was looking through this the other day, I felt like she wanted to share His Word with you girls. So, I prayed about it, selected four of them, and had them scanned, enlarged, printed, and framed.

"Because," Dad continued, "your mother may be with the Lord now, but Scripture tells us that the Lord is with us always. That means if *He* is with *us* and *she* is with *Him*, then *she* is with *us* too. And she is definitely with us when we are praising and loving God and each other and . . ." he gestured at our presents, "sharing His Word."

Lena nodded as she smiled down at her verse, which read in Mom's feminine, loopy style, "'For I know the plans I have for you,' declares the LORD, 'plans to prosper you and not to harm you, plans to give you hope and a future.'"—Jeremiah 29:11.

"Thanks, Dad," she said in a sniffly voice as she wiped her eyes.

"Yeah, thanks," I said, as I gently stroked the glass over my Scripture verse. A gentle feeling of warmth blossomed around my heart and seemed to bloom out of me like invisible vines to encircle my whole family. I suddenly knew what to do: I ran to my dad—almost bowling him over—to give him a great big hug. Then each of my sisters joined me and we all piled onto Dad like snowballs of love.

"Group hug!" Dad shouted, and we all laughed. Then I closed my eyes to soak up the love as we held each other for a minute. When I opened them and saw my present still on the table, I shouted, "Let's go hang them up!"

"Okay, let me just get the hammer and some nails," Dad said, and he headed for the garage, where he kept the toolbox.

Cammie slapped herself on the forehead with the palm of her hand. "I should have recorded this!" She whipped out her cell phone and jogged after Dad. "Wait for me!"

Cammie and Kitty were recording bits and pieces of our daily lives to send as videos to our grandmothers, who wanted to see how we were all settling in. This was a perfect project for the twins because they really liked making "movies" for fun. In fact, that was the reason Ashton was called Cammie. She used her cell phone mostly for making videos and had gotten into the habit of basically recording us all the time—even doing boring things, like sitting around and watching TV. It had gotten to be so much that Mom started teasing her by calling her "Camera Girl." Then after a while, it just became "Cammie" or "Cam." Ashton loved it because it had been Mom's special name for her. But now that Mom was gone, she wanted the rest of us to keep calling her that special name. And considering how often she had her camera out, it was easy to do.

As I watched her dash into the garage, I had to admit to myself that even though I had found some of the constant recording annoying at first, in the end I was glad she had done it. Now we at least had a lot of video of Mom we could watch whenever we wanted.

Dad was in my room a little while later (without Cammie, who had already recorded him in her room). I watched as he used a level to make sure he was hanging the picture straight. Then, with a nod of satisfaction, he pounded the nail neatly into the wall with three blows.

As I watched him straighten the frame on the wall, I reread the Scripture, "The joy of the LORD is your strength," and wondered why he had chosen *that* Scripture for me.

"Dad?"

"Hmm?" He turned to look at me just as his phone went off. "It's your Aunt Samantha," he said just as I saw her photo and name come up on the screen of his phone. "I've got to take this." He stepped away and said, "Hey, Sis . . ." After they spoke for about five minutes, he hung up, quickly put the hammer back in the toolbox, and said, "Round up the others. We have to finish getting ready for your aunt's arrival. She'll be here very soon."

I slapped myself on the forehead. Our dad's big sister was moving in with us, and the four of us girls had all been working on different ways to welcome her. *I* was cooking up something special. Something warm. Something sweet and (I thought, once I heard the oven timer go off) something *ready*! I rushed down to the kitchen.

Chapter 2

When I hit the landing, I took in a long, deep breath. The homey scents of baking bread and cinnamon combined and filled the first floor. *Heaven must smell a little bit like this,* I thought, and headed for the stove.

I bent down and peeked through the window of the oven. The cinnamon rolls had fattened and browned nicely. They were done. I grabbed my pink and blue unicorn apron and matching oven mitts from their hooks and slipped them on. Then I carefully slid the tray of piping hot cinnamon rolls out of the oven. They smelled even more amazing once they were out on the counter. I could hardly wait to have some—I felt saliva fill my cheeks. But first I had to make the glaze.

I quickly grabbed a large bowl and poured powdered sugar, butter, cream cheese, and vanilla into it. I used a whisk to blend them together, adding warmed milk a little at a time to make the glaze runny enough. When the icing was done, I drizzled it over the tops of all the rolls, and the sweet vanilla-cream-cheese-sugar smell combined with the cinnamon smell to create an even more incredible aroma. I admired the tray of glistening sweets and licked my lips. *Perfect!*

I looked up with a proud smile but . . . there was no one around to smile back at me. Mom and I used to bake together all the time. It was one of those special mother-daughter activities that she and I would do at least once a week. Baking wasn't the same without her. My shoulders sagged.

But missing Mom wasn't the only thing that was bothering me. *Where is everybody?* I wondered. Usually by the time my cinnamon rolls were done, their aroma would draw family members into the kitchen from all different corners of the house. Then my sisters and I would argue over who had dibs on one of the middle rolls (they were the fluffiest and best). Even though I had already decided that today those rolls would be going to Aunt Samantha, I was still disappointed to find that I was not surrounded by drooling fans. Even Austin, our blue-nosed American bully, was nowhere to be found, and the kitchen was his favorite place to hang out.

"Hey! Doesn't anybody smell this?" I called out.

Just then I heard the footfalls of the twins (as well as a set of four paws) coming down the stairs. The girls were each holding on to the end of a banner they had made with colored sheets of paper cut into triangles. On each triangle was a letter made of sparkly washi tape that spelled the word "WELCOME!" (Exclamation point included.)

"We need to put this up!" Kitty said breathlessly. She jumped up and down. "She'll be here any minute!"

"Where's Dad?" Cammie added, craning her neck to look through the French doors of his office.

Austin ran around them, hopping on his back legs and looking like he wanted to try to hang up the banner for them. His excited barks were probably doggy language for "I help! I help!"

"Here I am, girls! We'll hang this over the dining room entryway, so she can see it when she comes in," Dad said.

Lena came down the stairs with another sign. "You almost

forgot this," she told the twins. It was another fluttering banner made up of smaller triangles. This time they spelled out the names "AUNT SAMANTHA & ZETTE!"

While Dad began stringing it up under the first banner, Cammie handed the camera phone to Kitty. "Film this!" she commanded, and she picked up Austin's front paws and began to dance with him. "Are you looking forward to having your bestie move in, boy?" she asked him, her voice pitched higher than usual. "Are you, boy? Are you? Yes, you are! Yes, you are!"

Austin's "bestie" was Aunt Samantha's French bulldog, Zette (short for Crepes Suzette). Austin and Suzette had been friends since their puppy days, so the two dogs really got along, which was especially good now that Samantha and Suzette were coming to stay.

A car horn honked outside. "That's them!" Kitty squealed.

Austin started barking while Cammie peeked outside from behind a window curtain. "There's a moving van too."

"Lena, put Austin in his crate for now. We'll have to keep the front door open when we bring Aunt Sam's things in, and you know how he likes to run off."

"Okay. Come on, boy," Lena said with a grunt as she hauled Austin away from the excitement.

The rest of us ran out to greet Aunt Samantha.

She had just stepped out of her car and was throwing her arms out in a stretch when she saw us. "Mmmm! That feels good!" she said. Then, putting her hands on her hips, she bent her body sideways once to the left, then once to the right. Finally, she twisted her torso back and forth. "Ahhh. I needed that!"

I got to her first, so when she finished stretching, I launched myself at her. She wrapped me in a warm bear hug. "Hi, Ansley, sweetie."

"Hi, Auntie Sam," I said, breathing in her signature scent. Aunt Samantha wore the same perfume every day. It was a light, lemony smell like magnolias in a spring breeze. "Where's Zette?"

"Oh, I let her out so she could stretch her legs too," she said, pointing behind me.

Zette scurried over to my dad and started yipping at his feet. The twins bent down and began cooing over her.

Dad waved at the mover's van parked on the street. "You can pull up closer," he called.

The man behind the steering wheel saluted and turned the ignition key. Suddenly there was a loud, popping sound, like a small cannon going off, and a puff of smoke shot out the back of the van. We all started at the noise, but Zette let out a terrified yelp and dashed down the street.

"Zette!" Aunt Samantha cried out.

"Oh, no! Zette! Come back!" I yelled and set off after her at a run.

For a short-legged dog, Zette turned out to be a fast runner. I could hear her panting, and I began to pant myself. *What if she gets lost and I have to go back empty-handed? What happens if I'm the one who ends up lost instead? I still don't know the neighborhood well enough!* My thoughts were running faster than my feet.

Then I heard my aunt behind me, calling her dog by her whole name. "Crepes Suzette! You come back here!"

But Zette did not stop. Instead, she barreled down the sidewalk, straight toward a pair of girls around my age who were sitting at a table with a big pitcher of lemonade, a stack of paper cups, and a platter filled with cookies.

My shouts turned to a whisper. "Oh, no." Then I yelled, "Watch out!"

The girls, who had been talking to one another, turned at the sound of my voice and leapt to their feet. One girl had been holding a metal money box on her lap, and it fell to the ground with a clatter and the sound of scattering coins. This just spooked Zette more, and the dog backed away from the box and into one of the table legs, knocking the aluminum table off balance, as well as the lemonade and cookies on top of it. I squeezed my eyes shut and pressed my lips together when it all came tumbling down.

The commotion she caused increased Zette's panic, and she came running back toward me and Aunt Samantha. I bent down and snatched her before she had a chance to run past us and create more chaos. Then I hurried over to the girls, my sandals smacking against the now lemonade-drenched sidewalk.

"I'm so sorry!" I told the girls. "Your lemonade stand is ruined."

The girls were picking up the money from the ground. One girl, who had a long, red French braid and freckles, had her mouth set in a grim line. The other girl, who had a blondish-brown bob with bangs, looked ready to laugh.

The grim-looking girl said, "It's okay. It was an accident."

The happier looking girl said, "Is this your dog? Are you our new neighbors?" And she began petting Zette on the head saying in a baby voice, "No, you can't have a cookie, silly doggy. Cookies are bad for you." Then her voice took on a more normal tone. "Well, unless of course, they're *doggy* cookies."

Zette's ears perked right up and her tail began to wag. She thought she was getting a treat.

"No, Zette," I said sternly, "those aren't doggie biscuits—and you *don't* get a treat for making a huge mess!"

Aunt Samantha finally caught up to us. "Oh, ladies, I'm so sorry," she said, and her eyebrows turned up at the sight she saw before her. "What a disaster! And I bet you baked those cookies too."

The redhead bit her bottom lip and nodded.

I handed Zette back to Aunt Sam and bent down to pick up the now-empty pitcher of lemonade. "Everything is ruined."

"Oh, it's okay," the girl with the bangs said, with a nonchalant wave of her hand. "I was getting bored of the lemonade stand anyway." Behind her, the redheaded girl crossed her arms. The girl with the bangs didn't notice. "I'm Krista, by the way. Krista Matthison. I live right there." She pointed at the house behind her just as a short-haired woman in a pink tunic shirt and white cropped pants came hurrying out of the front door, a concerned expression on her face. "That's my grandma, Hunni, and this . . ." Krista nodded at the redhead, ". . . is my friend, Taylor."

"*Best* friend," Taylor mumbled. "Taylor Lang."

"What's *your* name?" Krista asked me, and grinned widely, showing off aqua-and-pink-colored braces.

"I'm Ansley Daniels. This is my Aunt Samantha and her naughty dog, Crepes Suzette."

Krista squealed. "Oh! That name is adorable! And so are you!" She pouted at Zette, who wagged her stump of a tail.

I flashed Taylor a smile, but she wouldn't look directly at me. "I really am very sorry about all this," I said again, as Krista's grandmother came up to us, waving hello. "The moving truck backfired. The dog freaked out," I explained to her.

"I see, I see," she said, inspecting what used to be the lemonade stand. "I'm Krista's Grandma Hunnicut," she said, extending her hand to Aunt Samantha. "We were planning to come by a little later to welcome you to the neighborhood. We only just got back last night from seeing some family out west."

"Do you also live around here?" I asked Taylor, trying to include her in the conversation. But Taylor just shook her head.

My aunt dug into the pocket of her pants. "Let me pay for those cookies and lemonade." She took out a twenty-dollar bill.

Hunni pushed her hand away. "Oh, no, you don't have to do that . . ."

As the grownups went back and forth, trying to be nice to each other, I had an idea. "Why don't you two come with me?" I asked the girls. With Hunni's permission, the two girls followed me and Zette back to my new house.

Dad was still outside, directing the movers in and out of the house. "When I saw that you and Aunt Sam caught up with Zette," he told me, "I decided it was best to take care of this end of things. And who do we have here?"

I introduced Krista and Taylor to Dad and explained what happened. Then I took a deep breath. "And I figured . . . Dad? I think I know just the way to make it up to them. Would you be okay with me giving them what I was going to give Aunt Samantha?"

My dad's smile was soft and proud. "That sounds like a very good idea."

I grinned up at him, standing on tip-toe. "Thanks, Dad! Come on!" and led the girls into the house.

Lena and the twins were in the kitchen. I gave Lena the dog, and after introducing everyone and telling my sisters what happened, I slid my tray of cinnamon rolls across the counter toward Krista and Taylor. "I want you to have these," I said. "I'm sorry about the cookies. You can sell these if you want and try to make some of the money you lost."

I heard Lena take in a deep breath. And even though Kitty and Cammie were not identical twins, at that moment they both flashed me identical looks of horror. *Not the cinnamon rolls!*

Taylor blinked down at the tray, looking thoughtful.

But Krista shook her head. "Oh, we couldn't!" she said, sounding a lot like her grandmother, southern accent and all. "But . . . maybe . . . we could try some?"

At that moment, Dad, Aunt Sam, and Hunni came through the door, and with Dad's permission, I began cutting the cinnamon rolls and handing them out. The grownups sat at the kitchen table, chatting (although Dad, Aunt Sam, and sometimes Lena took turns jumping up and telling the movers where to leave things) while my two new friends and I sat on the saddle-shaped stools at the kitchen counter, getting to know each other. The twins ran back and forth between us and the grownups (sometimes recording all that was going on) and with their giggling, the dogs barking, the movers tromping, and the adults chatting, it got very noisy.

"So, you have three sisters?" Taylor asked, her eyes large as she looked around at all the excitement. She was almost cringing in her seat like a person adrift at sea with sharks circling her boat.

"Yup," I said. "Like Dad says, we're 'a foursome to be reckoned with.'"

Krista sank her aqua-and-pink-braced teeth into the fluffy cinnamon roll and got a little glaze on the tip of her nose. "These are awesome! Did *you* make these, Ansley?"

"Uh-huh."

"Wow!" Krista licked her fingertips. "She bakes even better than you, Taylor!"

Taylor froze midbite and stared at her friend over the cinnamon roll that was halfway in her mouth.

"I mean," Krista said with a cough, "she's *almost* as good as you are!" Then she grabbed the glass of milk I had just put down in front of her and swallowed half of it in five loud gulps.

I decided to change the subject, fast. "Do you girls go to Roland Lake?" I looked straight at Taylor to try to get her to talk. But Taylor wasn't looking at me again. Instead she was slowly putting the uneaten half of her cinnamon roll down on a napkin. So it was Krista who spoke for both of them. "Oh, yes! We're both starting middle school on Monday!"

"Oh, great," I said, relieved. "So am I. I was afraid I wouldn't know anyone there. It's scary to start at a new school where you don't have any friends."

"Don't worry," Krista said. "Now you have two!"

This time it was Taylor who coughed and took a long drink of milk.

I smiled at Krista. "Thanks," I said. While I really did appreciate her trying to make me feel better, I couldn't help wondering if she was wrong. That is, I wasn't really sure I'd made *two* friends that afternoon.

I guess I'll find out on Monday, I thought to myself, and sighed.

Chapter 3

After Krista, Taylor, and Hunni had gone back home, we got to work helping Aunt Sam get settled in.

Her room was on the third floor, with ceilings that slanted like an attic, which made it look very cozy. After we made her bed, put up some curtains, and helped her put away her clothes, we all gathered in the family room just outside her bedroom. It was where we kept a lot of fun stuff like books, puzzles, games, and art supplies and where the twins had made the welcome banners earlier in the day. With a TV, two couches, and a carpeted floor, it was a perfect spot for all of us to hang out at the same time. But the coolest part of the room had to be the chalkboard wall.

Dad had covered one wall with special, navy blue chalkboard paint that my sisters and I had a lot of fun drawing and writing on with different colored chalk. The first thing we did when the paint dried was to play a game of "pioneer school" with it. I couldn't wait to try more games with it, but when we all sat down, I noticed there was something new on the wall: someone had drawn a pair of opened theatre curtains on it.

Lena, of course, I thought. And when I saw her grab her guitar from behind one of the couches, pull up a chair, and set it in front of the wall, I knew exactly what she going to do: sing a song for Aunt Sam.

Lena smiled shyly. "I've been working on this for a few days. It's kind of short, but I hope you like it." As she began fiddling with guitar strings to make sure they were in tune, I saw Cammie borrow Dad's cell phone. Cammie pressed the record button just as Lena cleared her throat and began to sing,

Welcome
You are welcome under my roof.
Although to tell you the truth
You'll find things in disarray.
A lot's been going on,
And some of it's been tough,
But I hope you know that you're welcome to stay.

Welcome.
I open the door and let you blow in.
You knock things down, but your peace pours in.
Your wind will set things right.
Let it break through the clouds
Of our hearts and our minds
And carve out some space for the light . . .

Lena trailed off. "That's all I've got so far. But . . ." She shrugged. "Welcome, Aunt Samantha."

We all applauded.

Aunt Samantha got up from the couch to kiss Lena on the head. "That was beautiful. Your voice is so good! Right, girls? Doesn't your sister have an amazing voice?"

We all nodded. It was true. We had to admit that Lena sounded like a recording artist.

"Have you ever sung like that for Mallory Winston?"

Lena shrank back and shook her head vigorously. "Noooo! I couldn't do that. Mallory is a professional!"

"Well, call me crazy, but I think your voice is just as good as hers," Aunt Sam insisted.

Dad piped up from behind Austin, who was trying to fold himself onto Dad's lap even though he wasn't puppy-sized anymore. "That's what I keep trying to tell her. She's really good."

Aunt Sam went on, "I think God is calling you, sweetheart. Listen carefully to Him. If He wants you to bring people closer to Him through your music, don't let your fear stop you from following His voice."

Lena's eyes looked big and serious. "Yes, ma'am. I just want to be sure that's what He wants me to do."

Dad's eyebrows knit together in curiosity. "What's making you doubt? You said 'yes' to being in a movie a few years back and you weren't even interested in acting."

"That's just it," Lena said. "I *wasn't* interested in acting—just in meeting Mallory. But the movie kind of fell into my lap because God wanted me to have crazy faith and follow Him by doing something that I found difficult. But singing is something I really like. Something I really enjoy. Something I do for fun! How do I know it's something *God* wants me to do and not just something *I* want to do?"

Dad tilted his head thoughtfully. "Well, first think some more: were you able to help people by being in the movie?"

"Of course. It was a movie for God. It brought a lot of people closer to Him. When I met people on the tour, they told me so."

"Can't you use music in the same way? Doesn't Mallory do that?"

"That's true," Lena said slowly.

"And didn't you write that song?" Aunt Samantha asked.

Lena flicked a few of her long braids behind her back. "Yeah."

"If I'm not mistaken, wasn't that a song to the Holy Spirit?"

Lena brightened. "Yeah!"

"Doesn't that make your song a prayer?" Aunt Sam put her hands in the air, palms up.

Lena giggled into her hand. "Yeah," she said a third time. "That's also true."

My heart was pounding, and I sat up in my seat. "So think, Lena! When people hear your songs and learn the words and sing along, doesn't that mean they'll be praying and praising God?"

"Don't forget," Dad added before flashing Austin a look of resignation when the dog let out a loud snore, "the ability to sing, to write music and lyrics—those are talents. Which means they are all gifts from God. God wants us to enjoy life. The Bible tells us in the book of John, chapter ten, that God wanted us to have *life to the full.* He wants us to have joy and fun and be creative while we're on Earth. And in many places in the Bible, there are reminders about how good it is to offer God praise in song. Like in Psalm 95, where it is written:

Oh come, let us sing to the LORD;

let us make a joyful noise to the rock of our salvation!

Let us come into his presence with thanksgiving;

let us make a joyful noise to him with songs of praise! (ESV)

Dad's eyes were shining now. "God gives all of us talents to use in our lifetime. They are to help us enjoy His creation, and to help our neighbors, as well. He *expects* us to use those talents. Like in the Parable of the Talents in Matthew 25."

"I thought the talents in the Bible were a kind of money," I said, and twisted my mouth into the size of a button.

"They were," Dad said. "But the word 'talents' also means abilities or skills. When the master gives talents to his servants, he expects them to be invested, so that the money grows and they can give him the profit when he returns. It's their job to make more out of what he gives them.

"But if you see the master in the story as *God*, and the servants as *us*, or mankind, then the story is saying that God gives us all special skills and abilities and that He expects us to make something of them—something good that will make us and others happy. If you can paint pictures, then you should make paintings. If you can sing, you should sing songs. If you can write stories, you should do so . . ."

"All we're saying is," Aunt Sam said, "that you should probably let Mallory hear you sing one of these days."

"Yes! Do it! Do it!" Cammie and Kitty chimed in.

"One of these days," Lena said, looking shy again.

"Don't push her," Dad told the twins. "In the end, we all have to make our own decisions about things like this because God gave us all free will. He never forces us to do anything. So, if God doesn't, we shouldn't force anybody else either."

"I'll definitely pray about it." Lena got up from her chair. "Now I'm going to put the guitar back in my room."

Once Lena left, the twins looked under the coffee table at the selection of puzzles we had stashed there. "Can we start one?" Cammie asked Dad. They each took hold of one end of the same box and slid it out. It was a snowy outdoor scene that showed people ice-skating, sledding, and throwing snowballs. It was called "Winter's Paradise."

"Interesting choice for the end of summer," Dad said, raising his eyebrows in surprise.

"It's just so hot out. This will cool us off," Kitty said seriously. Then she laughed at the silliness of her explanation.

After Dad agreed, Kitty and Cammie shook the puzzle pieces out on top of the coffee table and Cammie said, "I'm good at puzzles."

"You mean you're *talented* at putting puzzles together!" Kitty teased her and laughed some more.

As the girls got started, I slipped out of the room and followed Lena down the stairs. I watched as she returned to her room and hung her guitar back up on her wall. Then she turned around with a questioning look. She must have heard me behind her.

I shrugged. "I just want to say you *are* really good," I said. "You *do* know that, don't you?"

"I guess I do," Lena said. "But it's the whole, 'singing for Mallory' stuff that makes me feel weird."

"Why?"

"I'm not sure." Lena sat on her bedspread and stared at the guitar that seemed to be quietly staring back at her. "Maybe it's because when I think of Mallory, I think of Mom."

I felt a pang in my chest when she said that but let her go on.

"You know, Mom traveled with me and stayed with me the whole time I was filming *Above the Waters*. But now, Mom's gone. And I'm not making any more movies or touring with Mallory. In fact, the last time we even saw or spoke to Mallory was at Mom's funeral. I don't know . . . I kind of feel like without Mom, there shouldn't be any more Mallory stuff. Like that chapter of my life is closed."

My shoulders sagged. "Oh." While I didn't really agree with her, I also kind of understood how she was feeling.

"But like I said, I'll pray about it." Her eyes flickered at the prayer journal lying on her desk. "I mean, if it's something God wants me to do, then I want to do it."

"Do you want to pray about it now?" I asked, stepping toward her and holding out my hands. "We can do it together."

"Okay." Lena took my hands in hers.

I closed my eyes. "Dear God, my sister and I come before you in prayer today to ask for your guidance. Please let Lena know what you would like her to do with her singing and songwriting. She only wants to do your will. Please clear the confusion from her mind and heart and help her to know what would please you the most. Amen."

"Amen," Lena said. She smiled sweetly at me. "That was very cool of you. Thanks, Ansley."

"You're welcome!" I said. I let go of her hands and headed back toward the upstairs family room. "Don't worry," I said, boldly. "God will let you know what He wants you to do soon." I felt very confident about it, and my heart was feeling much lighter about her situation. As I practically skipped back up the stairs, I had a sudden thought that made me stop near the top. *Lena has done a movie for God, and now she's doing music for God. She's got talents of singing and acting and writing. But what about me?* I wondered. *I don't act or sing or play an instrument. Dad said God gave* everyone *talents and that He expects us to use them. But . . . what are* my *talents? And how does God want me to use them?* I took a deep breath as I entered the family room. *I sure hope that when God tells Lena what to do, He'll give me a few hints too!*

Chapter 4

The next morning, I woke up in the middle of a wonderful dream about unicorns. Usually I hate it when that happens. I want to go back to my dream world! But this time at least I woke up to something that was *also* wonderful: the delicious smells of bacon, eggs, pancakes, and coffee!

I sat up for a moment and took a deep breath. "Mmm!" Then I threw off my covers and rushed down to the kitchen. There I found my aunt bustling around the stove, pouring out perfect, sizzling circles of pancake batter onto a griddle. Behind her, laid out on a tray on the counter, were amazing-smelling and still-simmering strips of bacon. I slowly reached out for one.

"Not yet!" my aunt said without turning around. "They're still too hot! They'll be ready in a few minutes."

I drew my hand away with a guilty giggle and squinted at the back of her head to make sure there wasn't an extra set of eyes peering out from behind her hair.

She flipped a pancake over and I marveled at how it was just the right shade of golden brown. Aunt Sam knew how to cook! With this thought, I noticed the eggs, milk, flour, and mixing bowl that were out on the counter, next to the bacon. "Aunt Sam? Are you going to bake something?"

"Yes. Some cupcakes for after church. Your Dad said we're all going to a barbecue at the pastor's house this afternoon."

"We are?" I trotted over to her side and reached for my unicorn apron. "I can help . . ." I trailed off as my hand met air. My apron wasn't on its hook. Neither were my unicorn oven mitts. Where had they disappeared to? I turned my head all around to scan the area as quickly as possible. *Not there . . . not there . . . not there . . .*

"That's okay, honey. Just go get your sisters before the food gets cold."

She slid some pancakes onto a dish, and when she turned to put them on the table, I noticed that she was wearing a checkered apron. What had she done with my—

"Go on, Ansley! Get your sisters!"

"Yes, ma'am," I said. I walked backwards out of the kitchen, blinking rapidly, then turned and obeyed.

The rest of the morning was noisy and busy as we all gathered to eat our hearty breakfast around the kitchen table. Aunt Sam didn't seem to sit still for a minute. She kept jumping up to either make someone more eggs, bacon, or pancakes or to check on the cupcakes or try to calm Zette and Austin, who were running around the table begging each of us for bacon. I didn't want to ask her about my apron and mitts in front of everyone, so I ended up sinking deeper and deeper in my chair while everyone else crowed about how yummy everything was and how glad they were that Aunt Sam had come to live with us. *I love her and her cooking, too,* I thought, *but now that she's here, does that mean I don't get to cook anymore? Am I banished from the kitchen or something?*

And I didn't feel any better about it later when I was just putting my dish in the dishwasher and saw Aunt Sam taking the cupcakes out of the oven. "Ooh!" I said. "Let me frost them, Aunt Sam, please!"

"Not today, sweetheart. They need to cool, and you need to go and change for church. It's your first Sunday there and you don't want to be late."

"I know, but—"

My father called from his room upstairs, "Girls! Get dressed, please! We need to head out soon!"

With a sigh that was as quiet as I could make it, I obeyed my dad and trudged back up the stairs. But I didn't like the uneasy feeling I had in my stomach. I tried to rub it away, but it sat there, and I knew that the only way to get rid of it would be to talk to Aunt Samantha as soon as I could.

Our new church was a huge, white building that reflected the sun. Walking through the front doors of the main building made me feel a bit like I was walking through the gates of heaven.

Everyone there welcomed us with smiles as they rushed this way and that. They all seemed to have places to go. I had the feeling that the angels in heaven were a little like that too. They probably all had jobs that kept them busy as they happily zipped between heaven and earth. I was beginning to feel a little bit lost in all the hustle and bustle until a tall blond man walked toward us, trailed by three blonde girls. He shook hands with Dad and told us that he was Pastor Dennis Whittaker and that the girls were his daughters. They ran up to us.

The eldest one spoke first. "I'm Nikki," she said with a grin. She had the longest hair of the three—almost to her waist—and was the darkest blonde of the sisters. She looked to be about my age. "I can show you where to go for worship," she said to me.

Her younger sisters waved at the twins. "And you can follow us!"

"I hope you like music, Lena," Pastor Dennis said, gesturing for her and Dad to follow him. "Because in Teen Worship there will be a lot of singing today."

I exchanged looks and smiles with Lena before we went our separate ways. *That was fast,* I thought to myself. *Looks like God is trying to tell Lena something already!*

"Sometimes we do music too," Nikki told me as she led me to a room that looked like a small theater. "But we also do arts and crafts and games and Bible discussions. You'll see."

I was in a group of middle school kids that ended up reading from First Corinthians chapter twelve about how many parts make up one body. Then we discussed how it was like the church since many people make up the one church and how different people participate in different ways to make it run, the way all the different body parts work together. Then we got to act in a little play where a bunch of us pretended to be parts of the body (I was an ear) arguing over who was the most important. Of course, the play ended on the idea that what was most important was how we all worked *together* to help the body be its best.

I had to say the line, *"What* did you say . . . ?" about ten times. By the fifth time I couldn't say it without giggling, and by the time the play was over I was laughing so hard I was crying. It was a very fun way to discuss an important idea.

When the service was over, Nikki bounced over to me and

said, "Are you coming for lunch? We've got a trampoline in the backyard!"

I turned to her with wide eyes and shouted, "*What* did you say . . . ?" and this made us both laugh so hard we had to lean on each other to not fall down.

When I met up with the rest of my family, I grabbed Cammie to tell her about the trampoline—she loves them! She was so excited by the news that by the time we arrived at the Whittaker's, she was the first person in the Daniels family to go through the gate to their backyard. Once inside, she grabbed Lena's hand and practically dragged her over to the trampoline.

Other church families were also there, and most of them had gathered around the picnic tables that were practically sagging under all the food laid out on top of them. There were coolers of icy canned drinks, bowls of homemade punch, freshly grilled burgers and hot dogs, platters of cookies, and just about every kind of pie (with every kind of crust) you could think of.

But Kitty and I bypassed the food. Instead we followed the Whittaker girls around as they gave us a tour of their backyard. They had a lot of things set up besides the trampoline, like monkey bars, a soccer net, and a basketball hoop. *Looks like we're dealing with a pretty sporty set of sisters,* I thought to myself.

But the one sports-related object in their yard that drew my attention the most was a long, straight beam, sitting low to the ground. "Is this a balance beam?" I asked. I heard my voice go all squeaky.

Nikki whirled around to face me, and her hair whipped behind her like a streamer. "Yes! How did you know?"

"How?" I leapt onto it. Then, after a thoughtful pause, I did a quick jump in the air, bending at the waist while folding my left leg so that my toes pointed down and jutting my right leg straight out so that my toes pointed out in front of me. Then I landed neatly back on the beam. I followed that maneuver with a backflip, and I ended with another firm and precise landing on the beam.

Nikki, her sisters, and other guests at the party applauded. I hadn't realized so many people had been watching. "A wolf jump and a back tuck!" Nikki announced, her eyes wide.

I nodded. "I used to take gymnastics in my old neighborhood," I said while walking up and down the beam. Then I threw in a couple of split jumps.

Nikki watched me, her face ecstatic. "You *have* to join my gym, Ansley! Grace-n-Power Gymnastics. It's the best there is. The coaches are great. You can join our team and compete and everything!"

I clasped my hands together and smiled open-mouthed at her. "That would be awesome!"

Just when I said that, Dad and Pastor Whittaker strolled over holding paper plates loaded with food.

"Don't you girls want anything?" Pastor Dennis asked, waving a hot dog.

His daughters converged on him like baby birds surrounding their mother bird who was offering them a fresh worm.

Staying on the balance beam, I reached over and tugged at my father's sleeve. "Daddy! Daddy! Can I join Nikki's gym? Oh, please-oh-please-oh-pretty-please?" I made my eyes as big and pleading as I could.

"You mean like for gymnastics? Like you used to? I don't see why not," Dad said.

"Yes!" I punched the air.

"But if you're going to be a gymnast, you're going to have to make sure you eat some protein for muscle strength and strong bones," Dad said, waving a hamburger at me teasingly.

"Thanks," I said. "I'm starving." I snatched it.

"Share with Kitty," Dad reminded me.

As I tried to break the burger into two even pieces, Dad gestured towards the tables and said, "Girls, don't forget to try some of your aunt's yummy cupcakes before they're all gone."

I stopped mid-chew, suddenly remembering my missing apron and not being able to help in the kitchen that morning. I swallowed hard. "Dad? Where's Aunt Samantha?"

Dad pointed toward the tables.

I gave Kitty her half of the burger and announced to the others, "I'll go get us some cupcakes!" And I rushed off before anyone else could join me.

I found my aunt standing behind one of the tables, handing out drinks, napkins, and of course, cupcakes. They were covered in pink frosting and sprinkles and, I had to admit, they looked really good. I walked up to ask her about my apron. As I opened my mouth to speak, I stopped myself. She looked happy to see how many people were taking the cupcakes and telling her how delicious they were. Her face was shining.

I set my mouth in a firm line. *This doesn't seem like the right time to talk to her, either,* I thought. Then I was startled by a voice directly behind me.

"Did *you* make those cupcakes, Ansley?" Taylor Lang asked me. "Or did your mom?"

Chapter 5

"You mean my *aunt?*" I peeked at Taylor from the corner of my eye. She was watching Aunt Samantha with a slightly bored expression on her face. *Does Taylor even know about my mom?* I wondered. It didn't look like it. It looked more like she had mistaken my aunt for my mother. "That's my Aunt Samantha, remember? I told you yesterday."

"Aunt, Mom," Taylor waved her hand. "Whatever."

I gritted my teeth at that but decided to let it slide. "Anyway, yes, my Aunt Samantha made those cupcakes."

"Oh." Taylor crossed her arms. "Lucky your dog isn't around to ruin them."

"You mean my *aunt's* dog," I reminded her. "Not mine."

"Right." Taylor shrugged.

I stepped toward the table where my aunt was standing and held out a dish. "Auntie Sam? Can I get a few of those?"

"Sure, Ansley! Hi, Taylor, honey. Would you like one too?" Aunt Samantha asked.

"No, that's okay," Taylor said, although she couldn't take her eyes off the pink frosting.

"If you don't want the whole thing, we can share one," I suggested.

Taylor brightened. "Okay. Let's make a deal. I'll share one

of these with you, and then you'll have to try one of my grand-ma's," she said.

"Did your grandma make cupcakes too?" I asked, peeling the silver wrapper off one of the cupcakes.

"*Did my grandma make cupcakes?*" Taylor raised one eye-brow and smiled smugly. "Follow me."

She led me over to a table that held a bunch of desserts. There were a number of fancy, multi-layered, full-sized cakes set up on cake stands, all labeled with beautifully hand-lettered signs identifying their flavors (like Red Velvet, Hummingbird, Carrot, Double Chocolate, and so on). There were also other pas-tries like éclairs, cannoli, and cookies.

"Which . . . which ones did your grandmother make?" I asked, wondering if it was supposed to be obvious, but that I somehow wasn't getting it.

"She made *all* of these," Taylor said. She put out her arms like a preacher blessing a congregation.

"All?" I couldn't help raising my voice. "But these look like they're from a bake shop!"

"That's because it *is* all from a bake shop. My grandmother's! She owns and runs Lynda's Lovin' Oven."

"Wow," I said. "So you have professional bakers in your fam-ily. No wonder Krista says you're good."

Taylor narrowed her eyes. I was pretty sure she was remem-bering when Krista called my cinnamon rolls better than her cookies. "I *am* good."

At that moment, Kitty ran over to me and started taking Aunt Sam's cupcakes off my hands. "What's taking so long?" she demanded to know. A glowing Cammie and Lena followed close behind, fresh from jumping on the trampoline.

"I'm so hungry!" Cammie said to no one in particular.

"Have one of these," Taylor said, picking up a slice of sticky-sweet looking cake with crushed pecans on top.

"Um, thanks," Cammie said. "Is there any, you know, like plain vanilla cake, maybe?"

Taylor's face fell.

Lena went into big-sister mode. Not noticing Taylor's reaction, she put the cake down on the table and patted Cammie on the back. "You need something a little more substantial, first," she said. "Let's go get you a burger." She led Cammie away and Kitty followed.

Taylor stayed, staring down at the grass.

"I'll try a red velvet cupcake," I piped up, remembering I had agreed to sample something.

Taylor quickly snatched one off the table. "Sure! Here. Now tell me that isn't the most amazing red velvet you've ever had!"

I shoved half of it into my mouth immediately to show some enthusiasm. It *was* good. Was it the best I'd ever had? I wasn't sure. I didn't want to lie and say it was, but I didn't want to hurt her feelings, either. So I munched and made a lot of "Mmm" noises and flashed her a thumbs-up sign.

This seemed to satisfy Taylor and even seemed to make her a little more relaxed around me for the rest of the afternoon. She hung around me for a while until Nikki took us inside the house to her indoor gym. There were some uneven bars there, and when I ran over to try them out, Taylor wrinkled her nose. "I don't like gymnastics," she said plainly. Then she waved. "See you girls in school tomorrow!" and left.

Nikki didn't skip a beat. "Let me show you some of the leotards I've worn at our meets!" she said, and she led me to her room.

It was a fun afternoon. By the time we got home we were all tired, but in a good way. Dad let us watch a movie because it was our last day of summer break, but he made us all go to bed early so that we would be rested for our first day of school.

But as I lay my head down on my unicorn pillowcase, the morning's incident with my aunt came galloping back into my mind. My eyes would not stay closed. I couldn't sleep. Not without speaking to Aunt Samantha first.

I crept out of bed in the dark. I had to do it super slowly since my room was still new to me and I was afraid of bumping into things I couldn't see or remember were there. When I got out into the hall, I had to shut my eyes for a minute. The difference between the darkness of my room and the brightness of the landing was almost too much. I heard creaking footsteps coming toward me and had to squint to try to make out who was coming up the stairs.

"Ansley?" Aunt Samantha sounded surprised. "What are you doing up?"

"I'm not sleepy," I said, rubbing my eyes to relieve them from the stabbing glare of the lights.

My aunt's smile was half-doubtful, half-understanding. "Well, you best get back to bed so that you can be fresh in the morning."

"But I can't. Not without—hey! What are you carrying?" I was sure I had just spotted something suspiciously . . . unicorn-y . . . in her arms.

My aunt looked down at the stack of folded items she was carrying with a puzzled frown. "Laundry?" She held up an oven

43

mitt. "By the way, I washed these and your apron too. It looked like it had been a while since they'd seen the inside of a washing machine."

I felt so relieved at the news that I took one of the mitts and hugged it. "So you didn't throw them out," I whispered to myself.

"What?" Aunt Sam asked. "What are you saying? Why would I throw out anything that belonged to you?"

I looked up at her. "Can we talk for a minute?"

"Come on." She led me up to the family room next to her bedroom and sat down on the couch. She put the stack of laundry on the sofa cushion to her left and patted the empty cushion on her right for me to sit down. "What's going on?"

When I told her about how scared I'd been that she'd done something with my apron and mitts, her mouth fell open. And when I told her I'd felt, well, kind of "kicked out" of the kitchen that morning, she put a hand over her heart.

"Oh! You must have been so hurt! I'm so sorry! I didn't mean to make you feel that way!"

I felt my eyes grow moist and warm. "I know that now, Auntie Sam."

"Of course I'll let you help me in the kitchen—and bake things on your own like you did before I came. I wouldn't take that away from you."

"I love cooking," I told her, and I pictured myself in my younger days when Mom first showed me how to break eggs over a bowl. "It was something Mom and I had a lot of fun doing together. And now . . . now when I cook, well, it's one of the times that I can still feel close to her."

Aunt Sam sniffed and rubbed my back.

"You know," I said, tilting my head, "I never thought about

it before, but maybe my love of cooking is also something I got from *you!*" I tapped my chin with my index finger as I mulled over this new idea. "I mean, from Dad's side of the family. Maybe it's in my blood." *Like Taylor,* I thought to myself.

"I bet it is. You *are* a natural! Those cinnamon rolls were delicious!" my aunt said. "I'm just sorry we didn't have time this morning for you to help with the cupcakes."

"And I only got to eat half of one at the barbecue," I admitted.

"That's too bad. We'll have to bake something else together one of these days."

Suddenly I blurted, "Mom used to make us a surprise on the first day of school . . ." And I explained the tradition to my aunt.

She looked thoughtful. "I think the whole point of traditions is that they should be kept up. Don't you?" Her eyes twinkled at me.

"I do!" I nodded vigorously and rubbed my hands together. "And I want to help!"

My aunt got up off the couch and began guiding me out of the family room. "I'd love you to, of course. Only, you do realize that if you do, your after-school surprise won't exactly be a surprise anymore, right?"

"I don't care!" I said. "It'll still be a surprise to Lena, Cam, and Kitty!" I imagined the excited faces of my sisters when they came home to a treat tomorrow. I loved the idea of being the reason behind their smiles. (Not to mention being the one responsible for continuing our mom's tradition.)

But my aunt woke me out of my fantasy with this point, "If I have to wait for you to come home from school so that we can bake together, your sisters will all be able to see or smell what we're making, and it will end up not being a surprise for any of them, either."

"Then . . ." I could only see one solution to this problem, "why don't we make something *now*?"

My aunt took a step back. "Isn't it kind of late for you? And with tomorrow being your first day of school, I don't think that's such a good idea."

I shook my head. "But that's just it! It isn't late! We went to bed early, remember? And I can't sleep. And if we made something now, it would be a real surprise to the others tomorrow."

"I don't know . . . We'll have to ask your dad. He sets the rules around here."

I nodded. That was very true, but I also happened to know of a loophole in one of those rules.

The two of us went downstairs to my dad's office. When we walked through the French doors together, he looked up from his computer in curiosity. "What's up, you two? Something wrong?"

My aunt and I began talking at the same time. When he began to understand what we wanted to do, Dad began to shake his head. But then I reminded him of his loophole.

"Dad, what's your one rule about us staying up past our bedtime?"

"That you have to work, not play." He gestured toward his computer. "That's usually why grownups stay up later. I was writing something for work—"

"—and I was doing laundry," Aunt Samantha said.

"Isn't cooking work?" I asked. "Isn't feeding my sisters housework? I'll clean up afterward too. I really can't sleep, Dad."

My dad chuckled. "You should become a lawyer, Ansley."

I could feel my heart pumping fast. He was going to let me do it. I could tell!

With a sigh, he leaned over, shut off his computer, and announced, "Okay, ladies, if we all work together, I'm sure we can get something done in hardly any time at all. Then Ansley will be able to sleep and . . ." He patted one of my dimpled cheeks, "you can surprise your sisters the way Mom used to surprise you all. But . . . what will we make?"

I knew the ingredients we had in the kitchen, and I also knew that I wanted to make something simple, but special. "Blondies," I decided, "with chocolate chips. But first, let me just go grab my apron!"

Chapter 6

The next morning I took a long look at myself in the full-length mirror hanging on the back of my bedroom door. Turning around in a slow circle, I checked out my new school uniform from all angles and nodded. I looked ready for the first day of school all right! I smoothed down the pleats of my plaid skirt and smiled. I just loved the way the navy blue and forest green checks—the official school colors—looked together. Next, I flipped up the collar of my soft, white polo shirt to see how I liked it. I tilted my head to the left and squinted . . . then I tilted my head to the right and pouted. Finally, shaking my head, I tried how it looked folded down. I decided to go with down. Nice and neat. Next, I slipped on the navy cardigan. Cute, I decided, but it was too hot to wear just yet. I decided to wrap the sleeves around my waist instead. I took a deep breath. "Here we go," I told my reflection, and opened the door to my room.

"Kitty? Cam? You guys dressed?" I asked the twins as I knocked on their door. "Come on, we've got to eat!"

"We're ready!" Kitty and Cammie popped out of their room triumphantly. Both were neatly dressed in their school uni-forms, too, and Cam had her phone out, recording as usual. But Kitty had on a pair of sunglasses and a fluffy, white jacket. She made me think of a movie star going to a red-carpet event instead of a girl going to her first day of school.

It's Glamorous Amber, I thought with a secret smile. Her obsession with her fluffy coat was the reason we called her "Kitty." It had been a present from Mom last Christmas, and Amber had practically worn it every day since, even indoors. Sometimes she'd cuddle up with Mom on the couch and Mom would pet her and call her "my fluffy kitty," and Amber would purr. After a while, whenever she'd call for Amber, Mom would say, "Here, kitty, kitty!" And so, in time, the nickname just stuck, as nicknames do!

"Um, it's still August," I reminded Kitty. "That's why I tied my sweater like this. It's too hot to actually wear a sweater or coat."

"Oooh," Kitty's eyes zooming to my waist. "I like the way that looks."

"Yeah," Cammie said, looking at my image on the screen of her phone. "I think I'll do that too!"

Both girls dashed back into their room.

"You guys!" There was an edge to my tone. "You don't have to copy me! I mean, we don't all need to be dressed exactly ali—"

But both girls popped back out grinning widely with their uniform sweaters hastily tied to their waists.

My sigh came out as kind of a growl. "Fine! Come on, or we'll be late!" I semi-stomped as I led them to the kitchen, but had to admit to myself that their copying me was better than having Kitty wear a winter coat at the end of summer. I didn't want other kids thinking she was nuts on the first day of school!

Lena was already downstairs, and we joined her for a quick breakfast of eggs and toast.

Lena was taking a sip from her tall glass of orange juice when she stopped, put the glass down, and sniffed the air. "It smells kind of nice in here . . . like . . . cake or something."

I choke-laughed into my glass. Most of the scent of blondies had been aired out last night. Or so I had thought. I threw a very quick glance at my aunt, who I saw was hiding her smile. I teased Lena. "Your *juice* smells like *cake*?"

Lena tsked. "That's not what I said." She smirked. But when the twins giggled, she joined in.

Dad finished his breakfast first. After hurrying to his office to gather up his things, he stood at the front door. "Let's hop to it, ladies. We need to get going!"

With hugs and thanks to Aunt Sam, we met Dad in the foyer. But before we opened the door, we automatically took one another's hands and gathered in a circle to pray.

"Dear God," Dad began, "we thank you for all the blessings you have given us. We are so grateful that you sent Aunt Sam to us to help out with the girls in our time of need, provide joy in our time of sorrow—"

"—and yummy food!" Cam piped up.

Dad nodded. "And yummy food. I also humbly ask your blessings upon my girls as they start a new year of learning in a new school. Help them to grow in wisdom, in stature, and in your favor as your Son did when he was a growing boy. Amen."

"Amen!" we all said.

"Tomorrow your Aunt Samantha will drive you," Dad told us as he led us to the car. "But since today's a special day, I wanted to be the one to do it."

As I watched him slide into the driver's seat, I closed my eyes briefly and thought . . . *and God bless Dad too!* I wished I had prayed that out loud earlier when he prayed for all of us. But I knew God heard the prayer that was in my heart.

As we drove along, I couldn't help but notice that my sisters and I weren't laughing and chattering as much as we usually did on our drives. I think we were all a little nervous about how the day would go and were lost in our own thoughts. Cam had a serious expression on her face as she quietly recorded everyone in the car. She panned the camera from Lena who was listening to music in the front seat, to Dad who was watching the road from behind the wheel, to Kitty who was looking out the window without really seeing anything that was going by, and finally over to me.

I sighed in frustration. "We're not even doing anything interesting! Can you put that thing away for once?"

Cammie looked a little stung. "I am documenting our first day of school and I want to capture a little bit of everything. Besides, even regular movies aren't all action, you know. There are quiet moments in them too. Right, Lena?"

Lena agreed. "That's true."

I hoped my dad didn't see me roll my eyes. Even though Lena had made one movie, I didn't think it made her an expert in moviemaking. Of course, it did mean she knew a lot more about making movies than I did. But *still*.

I pointed out the window behind Cam. "Film that!"

Cam turned the camera just as we were pulling onto the grounds of Roland Lake Christian Academy. As Dad drove through the gates, and the buildings slowly came into view, the scene looked like a shot out of some old-fashioned movie. The mansion, with its tall white columns, loomed majestically in the background while in front of it, kids in uniform milled about on the perfectly manicured lawns, running to each other and greeting one another with shouts, waves, and high-fives.

"Here we are," Dad said, shutting off the engine. "You girls ready?"

"As we'll ever be," I muttered.

We all got out of the car, said our goodbyes to Dad, and headed toward the school together. But right before we got too mixed into the crowd, Lena held us back and gestured for us to huddle. Thrusting her hand in the middle of our circle, she said in an almost-whisper, "Before we split up into our separate buildings, don't forget—even in times when we're apart . . ."

And the rest of us, placing our hands together, joined in, ". . . the Daniels sisters promise with all our hearts that we'll always be . . ." and we chanted, our voices growing louder and louder, "Together *four*-ever! Together *four*-ever! Together *four*-ever! Together *four*-ever!"

Then we all raised our hands up and whooped. Our moment of sisterhood made me feel lighter inside, and I turned toward the school feeling readier to face the day.

Suddenly I saw Krista running up to me, grinning with her friendly pink-and aqua smile. She flapped her hand at my sisters in greeting. "Hi, Lena! Kitty! Cam!" Then she took hold of my arm. "Come on, Ansley! I'm going to introduce you to all my friends. Bye, Lena! Kitty! Cam!" She tugged me along and we headed toward the school building.

"Ooooookaaaaay!" I agreed helplessly and fluttered behind her almost like a kite.

"Here she is!" Krista said, depositing me in the middle of a small group of girls. "This is my new neighbor Ansley Daniels!"

I noticed a couple of familiar faces. "Hi, Nikki," I said, trying to catch my breath. "Taylor."

Nikki came forward and put an arm around my shoulders. "We're already friends," she announced to the group. She gestured toward a girl who wore her hair in two thick, black braids and had a thin gold chain on her neck with a tiny cross on it. "See, Guadalupe? She's the one I told you about. She'll be joining Grace-n-Power Gymnastics. Won't you, Ansley?"

I nodded, glad to see how Guadalupe's face lit up at the news.

"We can always use more team members for meets!" Guadalupe said. "Are you good?"

Her question sounded sincere. It wasn't a challenge, it sounded more like she was eager to get a strong team together.

I shrugged. "I can compete at our age level, if that's what you mean."

Guadalupe clasped her hands together. "Great!"

Nikki drew me closer to Guadalupe and away from the others. "We can discuss more at lunch—" she started to say when Krista broke in.

"Hey, hey, hey! Not so fast," she said, laughing. She pulled me back into the main group. "No hogging the new girl!"

I knew they were all just trying to be friendly, but I was getting a little tired of being yanked back and forth. *I wish they'd stop acting like I was made of rubber bands,* I thought wearily.

"But we need to discuss gymnastics," Nikki said. She patted my arm and nodded. "Let's sit together in homeroom."

"Oh, no you don't!" Krista said. "She'll sit next to me! Don't forget! I saw her first!"

"Actually," Taylor broke in. "I saw Ansley first. Her dog knocked over my lemonade stand and ruined—"

I held up my finger. "My *aunt's* dog—!"

"—And it's the cutest little French bulldog you ever saw!" Krista squealed. "And the name! Crepe Suzette! Seriously! How adorable is that?"

The girls in the group (all except Taylor) cooed.

"Oh! I want to see her!" said one.

"Bring her to school one of these days!" said another.

Taylor threw up her hands and started heading toward the front doors. "We'd better get going . . ."

"Ms. Johnson-Jones is our homeroom teacher," Krista said, walking by my side as we followed behind Taylor. Krista didn't seem to notice how her best friend's hands were balled into fists, or how Taylor was walking way ahead of the rest of us in quick, choppy strides.

Nikki jogged up to my other side. "Yeah, Ms. Johnson-Jones is young, and she's supposed to be pretty awesome."

"Cool. Maybe she'll let us pick our own seats," I said, "and then I can sit in between the both of you."

Krista and Nikki nodded at one another. "That just might work!" they agreed.

I felt my shoulders lower in relief. I didn't want my new friends fighting over me. *What a strange thing to find myself worrying about!* I thought. *Just a couple of days ago I was afraid that I wouldn't know anyone at my new school. Now—before even stepping foot inside the main building—I'm practically the most popular girl in Roland Lake Christian Academy!* I shook my head. *This day is not going the way I imagined it would at all. Are more surprises in store for me today?* I wondered, and with Nikki and Krista on either side of me, I crossed the threshold and entered the great hall.

Chapter 7

I did end up sitting between Krista and Nikki in homeroom, but I quickly found out that I wouldn't be able to do that in every class. Middle school wasn't like elementary school, where you stayed in one classroom for most of the day. Now I was expected to get up and go from one classroom to another at the sound of the change bell—and each teacher seemed to have a different seating arrangement! Even those who liked us sitting in alphabetical order did it in different ways. One liked to have the chairs arranged in rows, another liked to have her students arranged around desks in groups of six, and yet another teacher had the chairs of the entire class arranged in one, big circle.

And in Ms. Johnson-Jones's Bible class we got to do it all—first the long rows, then the breaking up into small groups, and finally even sitting in a circle. She kept us moving!

"Call me Ms. J-J," Ms. Johnson-Jones told us when we first entered her classroom. She was young, friendly, and on the short side. I thought the nickname suited her. "Sit anywhere you like, but keep in mind it will be the chair that you will sit in for the rest of the year for both your homeroom and your Bible class, so choose carefully."

I made a beeline for the front of the room. As a petite person myself, I preferred to sit in the front. And I made sure to find a spot where Nikki and Krista could sit on either side of me.

Once I got comfortable, I took a moment to admire the cheerful, well-lit classroom. The tables and chairs were all done in pale, blond wood, and the large windows offered a great view of the lush, green grounds and the cloudless blue sky (which happened to be the exact shade of blue as the accent wall at the front of the room).

I bet that even on grey, rainy days it'll still look like a bright summer's day in here, I thought.

Then, when it came time for Bible study, Ms. J-J opened a cardboard box that was sitting on her desk, took out a book, and handed it to me. "Pass it down, please."

Before I did, I gave the book a quick inspection. It had a soft, brown leather cover and gold-edged pages. Stamped on the front, also in gold, were the words "HOLY BIBLE."

I passed it behind me only to turn around and have another handed to me.

"Keep going," Ms. J-J smiled.

So I did, and did again, and again, until everyone had one.

That was when Ms. J-J said, "The Bible you have just received will be your very own for the whole time you are here at Roland Lake," she said. "So put your name inside of it right now."

The sound of unzipping backpacks and pencil cases could be heard around the room as Ms. J-J went on, "And I'll expect you all to take good care of them, showing the Word of God the kind of love and respect it deserves."

"Yes, ma'am," we all replied.

Next, she asked us all to turn to 1 Samuel chapter 3. She asked Nikki to read a passage from it and then asked if anyone could explain what happened in the story in their own words.

I raised my hand.

"Yes, Ansley?"

"Samuel is sleeping when he hears God calling him by name. 'Samuel! Samuel!' Only he doesn't know it's God. He keeps thinking it's Eli, the priest who is taking care of him. So Samuel gets up and goes over to Eli and asks him what he wants. Eli is confused because he didn't call Samuel, so he tells the boy to go back to bed. Finally, after this happens three times in a row, Eli figures out it's actually God calling Samuel. So he tells him, 'The next time you hear that voice call your name, say, 'Speak, Lord, for your servant is listening.' And that's what Samuel does."

Ms. J-J nodded. "Great, Ansley. Now before we go any further, I want you all to take out the blank journals you had to get for this class. Turn to its very first page, and in your best handwriting, please write . . ."

And she wrote on the whiteboard:

Speak, Lord, for your servant is listening.

Suddenly there was a clatter behind me. Taylor dumped out an assortment of bright markers and gel pens onto the top of her desk.

"Oooh," Nikki, Krista, and Guadalupe looked droolingly at her collection.

"Can I borrow one of those?" Krista asked. Taylor nodded, and soon her pens were disappearing into the hands of her friends.

I really wanted to borrow one, too, but I didn't feel comfortable asking her. I had the uneasy feeling that she might not want to let me. But Krista, who had taken two pens by mistake, opened her palm to show them to me. "Want one?"

"Sure, thanks." But as my hand hovered over her palm, I glanced over at Taylor. She wasn't looking at me—or make that, *wouldn't* look at me. I suspected she was kind of watching me and Krista from the corner of her eye but was pretending she wasn't. So I took the purple calligraphy pen and said loud enough for her to hear, "I'll give it right back."

As we wrote down the Scripture, Ms. J-J went on, "These seven words will be the theme of your first year of middle school. Let them be your motto."

Guadalupe raised her hand. "Um, do you mean we're supposed to *hear* God? How are we supposed to do that? I know Samuel could, but then, he was kind of special, wasn't he? We're just . . . ordinary kids. We can't talk to God like that."

"Hmm. Would anyone like to answer her?" Ms. J-J asked.

Nikki raised her hand. "I don't think Samuel heard God with his *ears*," she said. "I think it was more like, he heard God in his *heart*. I think that's how we *all* hear God. In our hearts."

Guadalupe looked unconvinced. "I don't think I've ever heard him speak to me. In my heart, or my ears, or anywhere. I've only heard *myself* speak to *him* when I pray."

Ms. J-J said, "I understand. And speaking to him is good. Prayer is supposed to be a conversation between us and God. But when we have conversations with people, sometimes *we* speak and *they* listen, and sometimes *they* speak and *we* listen. This year, I hope you will all learn how to do the listening part of prayer better. You can start by asking God to "speak" to you, like Samuel did. Ask God how you can serve best him."

"And one way to learn to hear him better," Ms. J-J said, "will be by journaling. We will have Prayer Journal Time every Friday afternoon after lunch when you will write in your journals about two things—the time in the past week when you felt closest to God, and the time in the past week when you felt furthest away. It's a wonderful exercise that will help you to recognize the voice of God when he speaks to you."

"Will that work?" Guadalupe sat up in her chair.

"If you keep asking God with sincerity and faith, he *will* let you know. Maybe you won't hear the answer in a voice, like Samuel did, but you will understand it in your soul."

I was suddenly aware of how hard my heart was pounding. *I would love to hear God speak to my heart!* I thought as I capped the calligraphy pen with a snap. *Then I would know what talents he wants me to use to serve him.* I held the pen out to Taylor, my hand shaking a little with excitement. "Here you go. Thanks!"

Taylor narrowed her eyes, snatched the pen out of my hand, and quickly stuffed it back in her pencil case. Then she tucked the case under her elbow—and out of my reach.

Ooookaaaay, I thought as I turned back to face the front. *I guess I was right about her not wanting me to borrow the pen. But why doesn't she like me?* I peeked over at Krista to see if she had noticed her best friend's behavior, but she hadn't. She was too busy looking over her pretty, new Bible. I sighed and cupped my chin in my hands. I had the feeling that my first year in middle school was going to be a series of highs and lows for me.

My mood was up by the time I got home, though. Dad had also picked us up from school, so when we walked through the front door and into the kitchen, Aunt Sam was waiting for us with the blondies artfully arranged on a platter.

My sisters threw their backpacks aside and ran for the kitchen counter.

"Why don't you put the backpacks away and change

your clothes first?" Aunt Sam said. "The blondies aren't going anywhere."

"Okay, okay," my sisters grumbled, but not too seriously.

As we headed to our rooms, Cammie suddenly doubled back, and in a series of moves worthy of a ninja, she slid into the kitchen, pinched a tiny corner off a blondie, and threw it into her mouth. "Mmm."

Aunt Sam shooed her away from the platter. "And you should all wash your hands too!"

"That blondie's yours now," Kitty told her twin. "Otherwise it's not fair to the rest of us who haven't had any!"

"Yeah, it's a crumb smaller than all the others now," Lena said with a smirk.

Laughing, but secretly agreeing with Kitty, I ran upstairs to change into something more comfortable—like one of my unicorn T-shirts.

Once we were downstairs again, Aunt Sam asked us each how our day went.

I told everyone about our motto and that we all had to start prayer journals.

Dad patted my shoulders. "Your mother would like that prayer journal thing."

"I have a prayer journal too," Lena said, pouting a little. "And the high school has a motto for the year too. It's 'Here I am. Send me!'"

Dad nodded approvingly. "From Isaiah."

"We have one, too, don't we Cammie?" Kitty broke in. "It's . . . it's . . . I forgot!" She broke down in giggles.

"I didn't," Cammie said. "It's five little words—'you did it to me.'"

"From the twenty-fifth chapter of the Gospel of Matthew," Dad said. "Verse 40. What does it mean?"

Cammie knew that Dad knew what it meant. He just wanted her to explain it to see what she had learned in school earlier. She poured herself a glass of milk. "It means that whenever you do something good for someone else, you are really doing it for Jesus. And whenever you treat someone badly, you are treating Jesus badly. So be good to people, and don't be mean to them."

"Exactly, Cam. Very nicely put."

"Yeah. It means do nice things like feeding the hungry." Kitty raised a blondie like she was going to make a toast with it. "Thank you, Auntie Sam!"

"Yes, thank you!" the other sisters chimed in.

"You don't have just me to thank for the blondies," Aunt Sam said. "They were Ansley's idea. She's even the one who really made them!"

My sisters gasped. "What?"

"When did you do that?" Lena looked genuinely confused. "How?"

I grabbed the front of my unicorn T-shirt and pulled it out like I was tugging invisible suspenders. "Secret unicorn magic!" Then I popped the last bit of my blondie into my mouth.

"They are delicious," Aunt Sam told my sisters, "but I think it's because there is a real secret ingredient that your sister and I use when we cook."

The twins leaned forward.

"Love, of course," Aunt Sam said. "When something is cooked with love, it's always delicious. Some people just love to bake, and sometimes the love of baking itself is what makes it taste so good. Some people love to make others happy, and that's the love that makes the food delicious. Some people love the particular people they are cooking for, and that's what makes the food taste so good."

I thought about that for a beat. "But I love my sisters *and* feeding people *and* cooking," I said. "Plus, I just find baking really fun."

"That's why these are so awesome," Aunt Sam said. "All the love! Although we've probably had enough of them for now." She pulled out some plastic cling wrap from a drawer. "I'll be making a pizza for dinner tonight using my special recipe for homemade crust. We'd better make sure you all have enough room for it!" She poked me lightly in the stomach.

I was practically salivating from the mention of the pizza alone. "Oh, I'm sure I'll manage somehow."

My sisters all agreed.

Aunt Sam neatly arranged the leftover blondies so that it would be easier to cover them. "You know, Ansley, at the barbeque yesterday, someone told me there's going to be a big bake off this coming weekend."

"Really? Where?"

"Well, apparently, this town holds a really big fair on their Founder's Day, or on the weekend closest to it. They have it on the school grounds, since it's one of the only places big enough for all of it. One of the highlights is the bake off, since it's featured on the local morning TV show. People even come from neighboring towns to participate."

"Oooh," I said. "Are you entering?"

"I'm thinking about it."

"Can you find out if kids can participate?" I asked her. "I mean, is there a junior division or something? Or maybe we can enter together, as a team."

Aunt Sam's face lit up. "I'll find out tomorrow and let you know." She slid the platter of blondies into the refrigerator.

"Great!" I said. I hopped off the counter stool and "stuck the landing" like a gymnast. That reminded me. "Oh! And what about gymnastics?"

"You're all signed up. I'll take you there after school tomorrow."

"Yessssss!" I slid into a split on the floor and threw my hands up in the air in a silent 'ta-da!'

Chapter 8

The next day I decided to wear my sweater tied across my shoulders. This time the twins didn't copy me—until after we were in the car. By the time we were on our way into our separate school buildings, we looked kind of like triplets. I didn't know whether to be annoyed or to laugh about it. So I settled on throwing my sweater in my locker with my gym bag before going to homeroom.

Having a locker out in the hall instead of a cubby in my classroom was a new experience. It made me feel kind of grown up to use it for the first time. I was just about to close it and twirl the combination lock when I heard someone call out my name. "Aaaaannnnnnnsssssslllllleeeeeeeyyyy!"

My name sounded louder and louder as Nikki, her ponytail streaming behind her, came closer and closer. Once she reached me, she clamped her hands on my shoulder. "You're coming today, right? Did you bring your stuff?" She panted.

"Yup!" I pulled out my gym bag (yes, it had a unicorn on it) and unzipped it to give her a quick peek at the two leotards, chalk, grips, hairclips, lotion, and snacks I had inside. "That black and green leotard is my favorite," I told her. It had long sleeves and a subtle rhinestone design on it. "When I wear it, I feel like I'm in the Olympics or something."

"Ooh, pretty," Nikki said.

Suddenly I felt like I was being watched. I jerked my head up and looked over my left shoulder. It was Taylor, standing a couple of steps behind us.

It wasn't like we were doing anything secret. In fact, I didn't care if everyone in the whole school—all three buildings— found out that I was going to gymnastics later that day. What I didn't like was the feeling of being spied on.

"Hi, Taylor," I said.

"Hi," Taylor replied dully. She pointed to the locker on the left-hand side of mine. "That one's mine," she said. "Can you let me through?"

I didn't really think I was in her way, but said, "Oh, okay."

"You're neighbors!" Nikki said brightly.

"Looks like," I said under my breath.

Taylor flashed me a tight smile. Then her smile widened, looking a lot more genuine. I started to relax and smile more widely in return when I saw that she was really looking at Nikki.

"By the way," Taylor said to her, "did your mother call my grandma? That is, are you coming on Friday?"

"Of course!" Nikki nodded. "I wouldn't miss it!"

"Great!" Taylor said. Then she waved in the face of a familiar-looking girl who was just walking past me. "Oh, Bethany!" Taylor started chatting really fast, "I-can't-believe-we're-not-in-the-same-homeroom-will-you-be-taking-art-as-an-elective-this-year-don't-forget-about-Friday-you're-coming-aren't-you?"

The Bethany girl couldn't seem to get a word in edgewise, but her "yeah" seemed to be the one-word answer Taylor was looking for. At least it satisfied Taylor enough so that she let Bethany go.

"Great!" Taylor squeaked. "See you Friday!"

I narrowed my eyes at her tone. The squeak in her voice seemed a little too . . . squeaky. Her voice was a little too loud. Even the way she was waving and talking seemed kind of hyper for Taylor. Was she up to something?

When Nikki and I began heading to our homeroom and I saw Taylor come running past us to grab another girl, I knew she must be.

"Hi, Stella!" she squeaked in that fake squeak. "Will you be coming on Friday? It'll be *so* much fun! You will? Oh, *yay*! See you then!"

I almost asked Nikki what Taylor was talking about. Just what *was* happening on Friday? But instead I held my tongue. I knew Taylor was just trying to make me curious, and I didn't want to fall for it. The only problem was, of course, that she *had* made me curious. Then I realized that Nikki had been chattering away to me about gymnastics the whole time and I had zoned out. "Oh, sorry, what was that again?"

"Oh, just that you'll love our coach—and our team—oh, and everything!"

"I'm sure I will," I assured her.

At lunchtime I sat at a table with Nikki, Guadalupe, Krista, and, of course, Taylor, who joined us last. She was just slipping into her seat when I asked Nikki, "So the fall session at Grace-n-Power doesn't really begin until after Labor Day, right? So will today's class be more like—"

"Are you two still talking about gymnastics?" Taylor rolled her eyes. "Get a life already."

Nikki looked stunned. "Gymnastics *is* my life!"

"Yeah, don't be mean, Tay," Krista snapped.

Taylor shrank a little in her seat.

"Go on, Ans," Krista said.

I lost my train of thought. "I-I was just saying, well . . . never mind, we can talk later. At the gym." I ripped a bite out of my sandwich and chewed way harder than was necessary to break down the bread.

Taylor watched me with the tiniest of smiles on her lips before she turned to Guadalupe. "So, Lupe, are you coming Friday?"

"I don't know," Guadalupe said. "I mean, I'm allergic to wheat. I won't really be able to eat anything there."

"Oh, we'll have something gluten free for you, don't worry," Taylor said. "*Please* say you'll come! It'll be so much fun!"

"You have celiac?" I asked Guadalupe.

Guadalupe nodded glumly.

"So you won't be able to eat *where*?"

"You know," Krista said, finger-combing her bangs over her forehead. "At Taylor's party on Friday. Since it's going to be at the bakery."

"Oh," I said, and I looked sidelong at Taylor. *So that's what she'd been trying to do this morning: let me know that she was having a party and that I wasn't invited.* I felt as though a hand had clamped over my heart. But I didn't want to show her that I was hurt. Instead, I smiled at Taylor and asked, "Is it your birthday or something?" I tried to sound polite, but not that interested at the same time.

Taylor shook her head and opened her mouth to speak, but Krista took over, "Oh, no, it's like the invitation said—it's just a party celebrating the first week of school. She did this last year too." Then a frown flickered on Krista's face for about a second and a half. "You *did* get an invitation, right?"

I looked straight into Taylor's eyes, but she quickly looked away and down at the bottled drink she was sipping. "I guess my dad must have," I said. "Or something."

"You'll love the party," Krista went on. "It's right up your alley. Her grandma closes the bakery and we all get to use the oven and make cupcakes and stuff."

I heard Guadalupe sigh on my left.

"And you should see what Taylor can sculpt with fondant! She's a true artist," Krista went on.

Taylor flushed with pleasure.

I didn't like to admit it to myself, but it *did* sound like fun to me, and I *did* want to try my hand at fondant if I could. I found myself wanting to go to the party very much. "Well, if the invitation turns up," I said, "of course I'll go."

Krista waved her hand like she was swatting a fly. "Oh, I'm sure you won't need it. Just show up."

Taylor twisted her mouth into a knot, but then tried to force her lips into a smile. She pressed them so tightly together, though, that her lips practically disappeared, making her mouth look like a hand puppet's. "No problem, Ansley," she said, finally. "I'll make sure my grandmother sends your parents the address—if you can't find the invitation, that is."

I winced a little at the word "parents" (plural). I didn't correct her, though. If the girls didn't already know about my mom, I wasn't ready to tell them just yet—most of all Taylor. "Okay, thanks," I said. "I'll tell my dad to keep an eye out for the invite." . . . *that doesn't exist*, I finished in my head.

Taylor changed the subject. "Anyone else taking art as an elective this year?"

"With you winning all the prizes?" Nikki asked. "No thanks! I'm taking drama."

"Maybe next term," Guadalupe said.

"Sorry, Tay. Art *was* my *second* choice, though," Krista said. She wrinkled her forehead so much in her apology that her eyebrows slid right under her bangs. "I'm taking creative writing."

"What about you, Ansley?" Taylor turned to me last. She looked almost afraid to hear what I would say.

"No, I'm not taking art," I said and hesitated as Taylor let out a breath of relief, probably. "Actually, I'm taking creative writing too."

Taylor crossed her arms and shot glowering looks at me, then at Krista, and then at me again.

Krista, who wasn't looking at her, clapped the tips of her fingers together in dainty applause. "Yay, Ansley! Do you like writing stories?"

"Oh, yes!" I nodded vigorously. "Stories, poems, plays. And reading them out loud or acting in them too."

"Too bad you aren't in drama with me, then," Nikki pouted. "We had fun acting in Sunday school the other day. Didn't we, Ansley?"

"*What* did you say?" I blurted out. And the both of us laughed for about a full minute. "Sorry," I said to the others, finally. "Private joke." I turned back to Krista. "Anyway, acting's all right, and I was thinking of maybe trying it next term. But first I wanted to try creative writing because I want to learn how to better communicate my thoughts and ideas through the written word *and* the spoken word."

"It just sounds like an extra language arts class to me," Taylor said making a face.

I ignored her. "We're supposed to read our stuff aloud in

class and critique each other and everything. Anyway, my dad thought it sounded like it would be helpful training for public speaking and stuff like that."

"Public speaking? Why? You're not, like, shy or anything," Nikki said. "And you speak fine."

"Yeah, but he thinks this class would be really good to teach me how to present myself when giving a presentation or telling a story on the radio or something. That kind of thing."

"On the radio!" Taylor scoffed. "Why would *you* ever have to be on the *radio*?"

"For your information," I snapped, "I've already been on the radio. With Mallory Winston."

There were gasps around the table.

"Mallory Winston!"

"She's my favorite singer!"

"How cool! How? When? Why?"

"You're lying," Taylor said, shaking her head.

"I'm not lying," I said. "Look for it online. It should be easy enough to find." I felt my nostrils flare as I charged ahead, "My big sister, Lena, was in a movie with Mallory a couple of years back. Maybe you've seen it? *Above the Waters*?"

There were *ooohs* and *ahhhs* around the table. "After they shot the movie, Lena went on tour with Mallory and I got to spend some time with her on the road. We had a great, fancy tour bus like rock stars," I went on. "And once I was even interviewed on the radio with my sister *and* Mallory." At this point I had tilted my chin up high and was sitting so tall in my seat that I was literally looking down at everyone else at the table. "Mallory's still a family friend. She calls us all the time . . ." I trailed off when I suddenly remembered that the last time I had seen or heard from Mallory Winston was at my mother's funeral. "Anyway," I shrugged. "It's the truth."

The faces of everyone else at the table looked either stunned or impressed. Even Taylor seemed to be at a loss for words. Then the table exploded as the girls all started asking me more questions about Mallory and if I had had any other cool "brushes with fame" to share with them.

"Calm down, everyone. One at a time," I said. But even though I was smiling, I couldn't help but notice the feeling of shame that had begun creeping up the back of my neck. Because even though it hadn't been my intention to boast about Mallory—I had just wanted to defend my father's advice about taking the creative writing class—by the end of my "speech" I had ended up sounding really braggy. *What's wrong with me?* I thought, cringing to myself. *I'm not usually a show-off. "Fancy tour bus?" "Rock stars?" "Mallory calls us all the time?" Why had I said all those things?*

I shot a glance at Taylor. She was the only one not jumping up and down and peppering me with questions. Her arms were crossed, and her mouth was pursed in an angle that made her look very disapproving.

The thing she didn't know? I was feeling the same way about myself as she was about me.

Chapter 9

By the end of the day, it seemed like the whole middle school had found out my family knew Mallory Winston. Students I didn't know were waving at me in the hallways and calling me by name. But I couldn't feel happy about being popular. I never liked the idea of people wanting to be friends with others because of who they know instead of because of who they are. Plus, I didn't like having so many people liking me when I wasn't really liking myself so much right now.

So I could hardly wait to go to Grace-n-Power Gym that afternoon. The moment I walked through the front doors, I let out a long sigh. The sight of the shiny gym floors, the smell of the powdery chalk, and the sounds of squeaking bars and gymnasts landing with solid thumps on mats filled me with both peace *and* excitement! I don't think I'd ever changed into my leotard so fast. I just needed to feel my blood pumping through my veins. Gymnastics had a way of helping me sweat out my problems and clear my mind.

The coach for my group was a man named Philip Well. Everyone called him "Flip" for short, because he had been an Olympic gymnast and could flip well! He told us that the lesson that day was really to help the new people figure out what groups they would best belong in and for the old and new members to get to know each other.

"Even though you will eventually be separated into groups according to your ages and abilities," Coach Flip said, "I want you all to think of everyone in this gym as a part of your family. Because that's how we roll around here. We help each other out. We want to see one another do well—even our competitors. We are here to build each other up, and to enjoy using the talents God has given us."

My ears perked up when he mentioned talents. And then he began our lesson with a prayer.

"Lord, it is written that our bodies are temples of the Holy Spirit. Help us to take good care of these temples so that we can glorify you through the work we do with them. Accept the way we use our talents as an offering of praise and thanksgiving to you and keep us always in your loving protection. Amen."

That's right, I thought to myself. I didn't really think about it before when Lena was singing for Aunt Sam the other day, but being a good athlete was just as good as being a talented singer. Just as a singer could praise God through their voice in song, an athlete could praise God through their body in sport. *Maybe this is it!* I thought. *Maybe this is the talent I can use to give God glory.* I started hopping in place a little. *Gymnastics takes discipline, commitment, and lots of practice. But so does any kind of work or art form you want to do well.* I could hardly wait to get started. But first I had a question. I raised my hand.

"Yes, Ansley?"

"So . . . would you say that the better we get at gymnastics, the better our offering to God can become?"

Coach Flip thought about it for a minute. "You *do* want to give your best to God, yes. But it's about the effort you put into it more than the result. If you try your best, that's the offering that's most pleasing to God. He doesn't care if you get a gold medal or a silver medal—or no medal at all. He cares that you are sincerely trying to learn, to improve, and to give him your all. Do you understand?"

"I think so," I nodded. "Yes."

"Great!" he clapped his hands together. "Show me what you got!"

I walked on the balance beam, worked out on the uneven bars, and demonstrated a floor routine that I had made up at my old gym. As I went along, Nikki and Coach shouted out encouragement—but so did other gymnasts I didn't know— even kids in different groups and their coaches. Coach Flip had been right about it being a family atmosphere and everyone trying to build everyone else up. Hearing all their cheers, whistles, and shouts for me seemed to make me do better and better. By the end, when I flew off the lower uneven bars and hit my landing, I was feeling pretty good about how I'd done.

Coach Flip looked impressed. "Yes. Ansley, you can definitely be in the Gracelets if you're interested," he said, which made Nikki do a little dance of joy, since the Gracelets was the competitive team that she was on. "But before we start our competitive season, we have a performance coming up. I'm going to see if we can work you into it somehow."

"Performance?"

"Can we just *show* her?" Nikki asked. And with Coach's permission, four girls around my age (the Gracelets) gathered together at the center of the gym. They were each holding these long wands with brilliant red streamers attached to them. They stood, waiting, two pairs of girls side-by-side and face-to-face. Then Coach Flip pointed to an older student. "Music, please."

She scrolled down a smart phone and pressed its screen. Suddenly, music by Mallory Winston started coming out of speakers in all corners of the gym. She was singing a praise song called *One-Three-Nine* about being "wonderfully made" by God.

I squirmed a little when I heard Mallory's voice, especially when Nikki grinned at me and flashed me a thumbs-up. But then I found myself caught up in their performance.

It was like watching a modern ballet. The girls did a floor ribbon routine that was incredibly synchronized, and the way they made the scarlet ribbons flutter, stream, and spiral looked downright magical. "How pretty!" I whispered under my breath. I also liked how each girl had a little solo to do so that they could have a moment to shine individually before all coming together again for the finale. When they were done, I clapped really hard. "That was great!"

The girls ran up to me, smiling and panting. "We'll be performing it at the Founder's Day Fair," Nicki said, wiping some sweat off her forehead.

"Oh, I wish I could join you! But it's too late," I said, hanging my head. "The fair's this weekend!"

"Maybe it's not," Coach Flip said. "Maybe we can work in a little part where you pop in, do a tumbling pass, and then pop out again. Not with a ribbon or anything, but at least you get to participate. How about it, girls? Want to give it a try?"

Nikki and Guadalupe each took one of my hands and pulled me into a circle made up of them and the other two Gracelets (a Gracelet bracelet). Then they jumped up and down, yelling "Yes! Yes!" to show me how pumped they were to make it all happen.

We used the rest of the class to work on the routine, figure out when the best time was for me to come in, and what moves I should do. "Come back again on Thursday and rehearse some more," Coach Flip said. "You'll see. We can make it work."

I certainly hoped so!

When class was over, as Nikki, Guadalupe, and I walked to the locker rooms to change, Nikki chattered away about the upcoming performance. "Just think, if we're really good, we could inspire other girls to take gymnastics too!" Her face glowed with both exercise and excitement. "And what did you think about our choice of music, huh? I thought you'd like that!"

I felt my face burn. "Yeah, of course I did. But . . . to be honest, I feel kind of bad about how I boasted earlier today about knowing Mallory," I blurted out. "I sounded like a show-off. It was awful."

Guadalupe's mouth dropped open in silent surprise. Nikki blinked hard a few times as she took in what I said. Then she shrugged. "I didn't think you were showing off."

"Well, I'm glad you didn't," I said with a sigh, "but *I* thought I sounded boastful, and I'm probably not the only one who thought so." My mind flashed back to the memory of Taylor's face. "Anyway, I think it would be better if we didn't talk about Mallory Winston for a while. Okay?"

I raised my eyebrows at Guadalupe to include her.

"Okay, but . . ." Guadalupe dropped her voice to a whisper. "We kind of have to say her name sometimes—like when we use her music for the performance."

I burst out laughing. "You don't have to whisper! I didn't mean that her name was taboo. I just meant . . . I didn't think it was right of me to use her name to make myself look important.

It was like I was . . . *using* her, like a thing, to make friends."
I sat down on a bench in front of our lockers and shuddered a
little. "But she's not a thing, she's a person—and a really nice
one at that."

Nikki sank down next to me. "I think I know what you
mean," she said, her eyes large and dark in sympathy. "You're
saying that you'd rather not talk about her at all than talk about
her to show off—or have people think you're showing off."

"Exactly." I was relieved that Nikki understood.

"Okay. Then I won't mention her for a while. But . . . don't
you think you're being kind of hard on yourself? She *is* a family
friend, right? You were on the radio with her, too, right?"

"Well, yeah," I said. I began lacing up one of my sneakers.

"So you were just telling the truth. It was just that you said
it in kind of an angry way because Taylor said you were lying."

I stood up. "That's something my mother was always warn-
ing me against," I said, hoping that Nikki hadn't caught the
"was" part of that sentence. "It's in the Bible somewhere about
human anger not being right . . ."

"'Human anger does not produce the righteousness that God
desires.' It's in the book of James," Nikki said.

"You know your Bible," I said, impressed.

Nikki raised her hands. "PK." She meant pastor's kid. "It
kind of comes with the territory. Besides, I think my dad has a
mini-poster in his office with that Scripture on it," she admitted
with a giggle.

"He does? Cool." Knowing that a pastor had to have a
Scripture reminding him to be careful of anger made me feel a
little better about myself. Anger could be sneaky. It could make
you do all sorts of things you regretted later. I wished I could

take back everything I had told the girls about knowing Mallory Winston. I didn't know her as well as Lena did, but now my entire middle school thought that Mallory and I were practically besties. *I sure hope people forget what I said about Mallory by tomorrow,* I thought as I closed my locker. But somehow, I didn't think they would.

Chapter 10

You got in!" my aunt said in greeting as I threw my backpack in the backseat and slid inside the car.

I nodded as I buckled my seat belt. "Yeah . . ." I gestured toward myself and the back seat. "I'm in."

My aunt looked at me through the rearview mirror and burst out laughing. "Of course, you're in the car, honey. I meant you're in the *Bake Off*!"

I covered my mouth as I laughed too. "I *thought* you sounded a little too excited about me getting in the car!"

As we continued to chuckle at my confusion, Aunt Sam passed a few sheets of paper to me. "I printed this stuff off the website for the fair. Take a look," she said and began pulling out of the parking lot.

I looked them over. Lettered across the first page were the words "Roland Lake Founder's Day Fair." And underneath was a big list of all the events, booths, and rides that were going to be there. It looked like it was going to be a big deal. The Bake Off would take place over both days, as Aunt Sam had told me before. It had two divisions (adult and child) and several categories (cakes, cookies, pies, etc.) that you could enter and win ribbons in.

"And on Sunday," I said reading aloud, "there is a grand prize winner for Favorite Cake of the Fair. The winner can be an adult or child! Cool!"

"Keep reading," my aunt said. "The grand prize isn't a ribbon."

"No, it's a trophy," I said, already imagining it taking up space on my desk, "*and* a spot on a morning show *Awake with the Lake!*"

"So, do you still want to do it?" my aunt asked. "It sounds like fun—but also a lot of work."

"It does. But it would probably be more fun than work—to me, that is. I mean, being on TV could be cool, and I'd love to win the trophy, but even if I don't, what matters is . . ." I suddenly remembered what Coach Flip had said earlier and gasped. ". . . is that I try my best and use the talents God gave me. It's just like gymnastics!"

"Baking is like gymnastics?" Aunt Sam sounded slightly confused and slightly amused.

"Yeah . . . I didn't think about it before, but they're both talents of mine. And by using them and enjoying them and trying to get better at them I can make God happy."

"Oh! Well, if that's what you mean, then I have to agree," Aunt Sam said.

Speak, Lord, your servant is listening, I thought as I placed a hand over my heart. "Now I just have to figure out what I'm going to make!"

"Maybe your sisters can help you think of something," Aunt Sam suggested as she pulled into our driveway.

"I'm definitely open to suggestions," I said.

At dinnertime I had a lot to share with my family. First, I told my dad and sisters about the Bake Off and asked them to let me know if they had any ideas for my entries (especially the cake). Then I told them about the upcoming gymnastics performance.

"When is it?" Lena asked.

I stared at her. "Oh, no! It's at the Roland Lake Founder's Day Fair too." I dropped my fork against my dinnerplate with a clatter. "How am I supposed to perform with the Gracelets *and* enter the Bake Off?"

"Now don't panic," Dad said. "We'll look at the schedule and see if we can work it out. They may not actually even run into each other. The fair is all weekend long and packed full of activities."

I nodded, but I didn't really listen to him. My mind was racing. Which one did God want me to participate in? They were both things I was good at. Both talents he'd given me that I wanted to use. But maybe he wanted me to choose one over the other. My breathing became fast and I pushed my plate of pasta away.

"Aren't you hungry?" Aunt Sam asked me, concern in her voice.

"Not really," I said in a small voice.

"The youth choir from church will be performing at the fair too," Lena announced. "I'm learning the songs to sing with them. I sit next to a girl in homeroom who is in the choir. We went over some of the songs at lunch."

"That's great, honey!" Dad beamed at Lena.

Yeah, it's great that she knows exactly what she's doing and isn't caught between two things the way I am, I thought as I crossed my arms.

"And what about you two?" Dad asked the twins. "What's new at school for you?"

"Well, we have best friends," Cammie said. "I mean, Kitty is my best friend of course, and I'm hers. But we've made friends with these two girls, Esperanza and June, who are best friends to each other. But also, at school, Esperanza is kind of my best friend and June is kind of Kitty's."

"Then we'll have to ask them over one of these days," Dad said. "Maybe on a Sunday."

At our old place, Sundays were kind of like our open-house day. After church, we usually had friends and family over for a few hours. It looked like Dad wanted to continue the tradition here in the new house. I was glad. It lifted my spirits to be around a lot of people.

Still, I was amazed at how easy it was for the twins to make friends so quickly and to be able to share "best" friends with another pair of best friends. There was no drama, no jealousy. Nothing like . . .

"Taylor doesn't like me," I said, surprising myself because I had spoken my thought aloud.

"What are you talking about?" Dad said. "Her grandmother contacted me today to invite you to Taylor's Back-to-School party at the bakery on Friday."

I smirked. "Only because Krista made her. She didn't invite me at first."

My aunt regarded me thoughtfully. "You just met her a few days ago. Maybe those invitations only went out to people she knew before she met you."

I didn't think it was worth it to explain how Taylor had acted earlier. How she'd purposely talked to people about the party right in front of me and how I was sure it was to make me feel excluded on purpose. Dad and Aunt Sam would probably just tell me she hadn't really meant it that way. Instead I just shook my head. "Trust me. She doesn't like me. I can tell."

"Well, then, do you even want to go the party?" Dad asked.

"Oh, yes, I do! Krista and Nikki and Guadalupe are going—and we'll get to bake stuff."

"Okay, then I'll RSVP for you," Dad said. "And maybe Taylor doesn't like you, as you said, but I bet by the end of her party, when she gets to know you better, she'll *love* you."

"Sure, Dad," I said, with a chuckle. Then I shot secret looks at my sisters that sent a clear message: meeting tonight.

That evening, after saying good night to my aunt and dad, Lena and I snuck into the twins' bedroom. It was a small room, with bunk beds and a navy wall that made the white furniture really pop. When the four of us gathered on the floor together, it was like being in a secret fort or tent. It felt cozy and safe.

"What did you want to talk about?" Lena asked as she folded herself into a cross-legged position on the floor.

Cammie and Kitty looked over at me with interest. Technically, I *had* been the one to "call" the meeting, after all.

I sighed before speaking. "I'm not sure, really. I just . . . I just wish Mom was still around to talk to, you know? And I figured, well, we've all got a little bit of Mom inside of us—"

"A *little*? We're all fifty percent Mom genes," Lena interrupted.

"That's true," I said.

"And Dad said that Mom is still with us in spirit, because she's with God and God is with us always," Cammie broke in.

"That too," I agreed.

Then Kitty jumped up, grabbed a framed picture of Mom from a nearby shelf, and put it down in the middle of us, faceup.

Seeing my mother's smile in the picture made me smile back automatically. It made me feel a little better. I looked around at my sisters. "I just wanted some advice. Mom advice. And I thought maybe if we all talked, we might be able to come up with some."

"What do you want advice about?" Lena asked.

"First, this gymnastics versus baking thing. Which one should I do at the fair?" I passed out the papers that Aunt Sam had given me. "Should I try for both? Or should I choose one over the other? What do you think Mom would say?"

"Pray about it," Cammie, Kitty, and Lena said at the same time.

"Oh, I will," I said, thinking about my prayer journal. "But what else might Mom say?"

Cammie drummed the fingers of her right hand across her chin. "Well, she might ask which one makes you happier? Gymnastics or baking?"

"Oooh, good one," Kitty said.

It was a good one. I closed my eyes and thought about the way it felt to bake something: from the process of putting all the ingredients together, to presenting it nicely, to tasting to see how it came out, to sharing it with people who really enjoyed eating whatever I made. I *really* loved baking.

Then I thought about gymnastics, from building strength and skill, to learning new routines and moves and then nailing them, to the final execution in front of a crowd of people who wanted you to do well and were fans of the sport. I *really* loved gymnastics.

I opened my eyes. "It's a tie."

"Then do both," Kitty said.

Lena nodded. "I agree. If you can, do both."

Cammie shrugged. "Maybe you'll like one more than the other when the fair is over."

"Maybe," I said. But I doubted it. "And there's another thing: Taylor. I don't know how to get her to like me. She was mad when Zette knocked over her lemonade stand."

"That would make me mad too," Cammie said. When we all looked at her in surprise, she said, "No, I mean, I love Zette. She's so adorable! But if I put in a lot of work putting a lemonade stand together and Zette ruined it, I wouldn't like it one bit."

"But it was an accident. And I've apologized a hundred times for it. But I don't think she's forgiven me."

"She doesn't have to forgive you," Lena said. "You didn't do anything wrong. It wasn't your fault."

"She sure acts like it was."

Kitty, who had been sitting with her back against the bottom bunk, hugging her knees and staring off into nowhere, suddenly asked a question that surprised me. "Do you really think she's still mad about that? Or is it something else?"

"What do you mean?" I was all ears.

"I just remember Mom saying, 'hurt people hurt people.' You know, how people hurting inside about something can take it out on other people. They want other people to hurt too. So that they are not alone in their hurt . . . or something like that."

Cammie joined in. "Yeah. That sometimes, unhappy people don't like seeing other people happy."

Lena finished the thought, "Like that famous saying, 'Misery loves company.'"

I squinted as I thought of Taylor. It was true. I didn't see her as a happy, smiley person. The only time she had seemed somewhat happy to me was when she had been inviting people to her

party. And that had been a kind of fake-happy. "That *might* be it," I said. "But if it is, how can I get her to like me?"

"I don't think we can make people like us," Lena said, getting up from the floor. "It's not something we can force people to do. Just be yourself."

"I *am* myself," I said. "And she doesn't like me. That's the whole point." I didn't get off the floor, and I was a little annoyed that Lena was already on her feet. We weren't done discussing my problem.

"Maybe you can help make her happier, though," Kitty said, also getting up. "If the problem is that Taylor's unhappy, maybe you can find a way to cheer her up."

"That's an idea," I said.

"Yeah, just be kind to her. Remember the lower school motto." Cammie spread out one hand and counted off the words on her fingers. "'You did it to me.'"

I picked the picture up off the floor and stood up too. "Thanks, guys. I mean it. I think Mom really would have told me the same thing." I hugged the photo to my heart. "But . . . why did we get up so fast?"

Lena put a finger to her lips. "'Cause I think I hear someone coming," she whispered.

We were all supposed to be in bed, not chatting in the twins' room. We all stood perfectly still. We were going to get caught!

Then the door to the twins' room slowly opened.

We all held our breath.

Then Austin ambled in, his tail wagging, to find us all together. Giggling, the four of us fell upon him, giving him hugs and pets and telling him what a good boy he was.

Then, leaving him with my sisters, I snuck back to my room

through the bathroom (since it connected my room with the twins') and closed the door. But right before I turned in for the night, my eyes fell on the Scripture in my mother's handwriting, hanging on the wall.

The joy of the LORD is your strength.

If God's joy is really my strength, I thought as I turned off the light and slipped under my comfy unicorn comforter, *maybe there's a way I can spread it to other people—especially those who really need it, like Taylor.* And as I snuggled down under the covers, my final thought as I was drifting off to sleep was, *Thanks, Mom.*

Chapter 11

Before leaving my room the next morning, I leaned into my mirror and slowly smiled at my reflection.

Nope, I thought as I pulled back with a "tsk." *Not very convincing.* I tried a bigger grin. *Nope again.* I shook my head. *Too toothy.* When I tried a third time, my mouth finally seemed right, but the eyes didn't. *The top half and bottom half of my face don't match! The mouth looks happy, but the eyes look serious. Hmmm. How can I fix that?* I tried crinkling my eyes to make them look cheerful, but when I did I could hardly see out of them! So I tried opening my eyes wider (without changing my smile) and ended up looking more terrified than happy. I couldn't help but laugh at myself—and finally smiled for real.

As I watched my laughing reflection, I told myself, *Remember how this feels and try to be this person when you see Taylor. Be so friendly and kind to her that she'll have no choice but to be nice back!*

I waved goodbye to my reflection (which I guess was kind of silly, but I had put myself in a silly mood) and was about to leave my room when instead I turned and grabbed a headscarf from the top drawer of my dresser. With its tie-dyed colors of emerald green and aqua, I thought it was very pretty—like the colors of a peacock. Whenever I wore it, it brought out the green in my eyes, and since the school colors were green and blue, it actually matched the uniform too. *This is just what my outfit needs!* I tied it around my hairline like a headband and knotted it in the front in a bow. My brown curls trailed out from behind it in what I thought was a pretty effect.

And then I whipped the scarf right off my head.

If the twins saw me wearing it, they'd probably want to wear bows in their hair too, I decided, and I stuffed the scarf in my knapsack. *I'll put it on once I'm at school.*

I felt a little guilty hiding it from them since I actually didn't mind their copying me so much. What bothered me is that they copied me *immediately.* If they would only wait for at least a day before imitating me, I probably wouldn't find it as annoying.

When I knocked on their door, however, there was no answer. *Are they really still asleep? It's only the third day of school!* I knocked a second time—a little more loudly. "Cammie? Kitty?" Finally, I used my fist as a gavel and thumped on their door. "CAMMIE! KITTY!"

"We're downstairs!" Cammie yelled.

Feeling my cheeks grow warm, I ran down to find them.

As I hit the last step, I caught the twins leaving Dad's office, giggling and nudging each other.

"What were you two doing in there?" I asked them.

They exchanged glances. Kitty spoke first, "We were just sending an email—"

Cammie jabbed her with her elbow. "Dad said we could."

I narrowed my eyes. The only people the two of them really emailed were our two grandmothers whenever they sent their little videos to them. And they usually sent them at night, like after dinner, or on a weekend. Not in the morning before school. "That's weird," I said.

"No, it isn't!" they practically shouted at the same time. Then they looked at each other again and went off into peals of laughter.

Kitty recovered first. "You're not wearing your sweater today," she said, clearing her throat and pointing at me.

I noticed she had her sweater tied around her waist and Cammie was wearing hers tied around her shoulders.

I shook my head. "Too hot."

Kitty shrugged. "Okay!" and she skipped away with Cammie following close behind, looking suspiciously like she was trying not to giggle.

Those two are up to something, I thought as I watched them head for the kitchen. I tilted my head. *I wonder what I would be like if I were a twin. It could be like having a live-in best friend . . .* I pursed my lips *. . . or partner in crime.*

Later that morning, once I was finally at school, I made sure to run to the girls' room before heading to homeroom so that I could put my bow back on. *I really have to get a mirror for my locker,* I thought as I rushed to tie the scarf. When I was finished, I couldn't help feeling like I had tied the bow better at home, but it still looked nice. *Besides, if I try redoing it now, I'll probably be late to homeroom*, I thought, and I hurried off to Ms. J-J's class before the bell rang.

Nikki ran to my side just as I was entering the room. "Cute headband," she said.

"Thanks!" I absentmindedly patted it as I searched the room for Taylor. She was already at her seat. *Smile,* I told myself as I strode up to her chair. *Look welcoming and friendly.* I nodded. "Hi, Taylor!"

Her eyes zeroed in on my head. "Nice *bow*," she said in a

voice completely different from Nikki's. Nikki's compliment had been casual, automatic, even. Taylor's was deliberate and firm and said with a smirk. "Wow, I haven't worn a bow like that since I was, I don't know, nine?" she went on. "Definitely before I hit double digits."

My smile dropped off my face just as my eyebrows pinched together. "What?"

"Aren't you afraid someone's going to think you're in the wrong building?" Taylor opened her eyes wide, like she was really concerned, but I knew she was just acting. "Someone might get you confused with one of your little sisters."

At that moment the bell rang for the start of homeroom. I sank into my seat without looking back at Taylor. I couldn't believe she'd been so mean about my bow. Did it really look childish? I thought it had looked really pretty in the mirror! I felt my right hand inching its way toward my head to take the bow off, but my left hand grabbed it and brought it down onto the desktop. I wasn't going to give Taylor the satisfaction of seeing me take it off. I wasn't going to let her words have that much power over me.

Then I heard whispering behind my back. It made me look over my shoulder before I could stop myself. I saw Taylor covering her mouth and speaking in a very low voice to a girl who was sitting next to her. It was Bethany, that girl she had very loudly invited to her party on Friday. They both looked over at me and snickered.

Are they making fun of me? I crossed my arms. *Why would they do that?* I turned to face front again, a scowl on my face.

The bell to mark the start of classes went off, and at that moment, Krista threw herself into her chair next to me, making her straight bob swing neatly. "Oops! Almost late and it's only day three!" She sounded both embarrassed and amused. Then, like Nikki and Taylor, her eyes went straight to my hair bow. I cringed inwardly, but she said, "Ooh! Nice bow! Pretty." Then she blinked when she saw my face. "Ansley? Are you okay? You look . . . mad or something."

I shook my head. "I'm fine." I didn't want to tell Krista what had happened for two reasons. The first was because Ms. J-J was calling the class to order. And the second was because Krista was supposed to be besties with Taylor. I worried that if I started complaining to Krista about Taylor's behavior I might be seen as a tattletale, or worse, a liar. Krista might even take Taylor's side. I cupped my chin in my hand and sat dejectedly in my chair. *And why did I want to be nice to Taylor in the first place? Should I even bother trying to be her friend when she so obviously doesn't want to be friends with me? Maybe I won't go to the bakery party,* I thought. *Not if Taylor's going to be mean.* I looked sidelong at Krista. She'd be disappointed if I didn't go, though. I sighed. I wasn't sure what I was going to do.

I still wasn't sure by the time homeroom ended and the change bell rang, but I was glad to leave and get away from Taylor, who had spent the rest of homeroom whispering and giggling with her neighbor.

My next class was creative writing, which turned out to be held in a classroom just off the library. This meant that we got to be surrounded by shelves of books, and everything smelled like dust, ink, and paper. On one wall above a low shelf of books were photos and portraits of famous writers. Above another low shelf were pictures of covers and illustrations from famous books including a beautiful painting of a unicorn.

The chairs (which were the kind with built-in mini-desks) were all arranged in a circle, and Krista and I found seats that were next to each other as our teacher introduced himself. His name was Mr. Doyle, and he seemed nice. He was older than my dad and had a soft voice, so we all had to be quiet to hear him well. He told us we were going to read a lot of books and write lots of stories of our own, not to mention poems and essays. He handed out copies of a suggested reading list he thought we should read as "future authors." I couldn't help hoping that book with the unicorn on the cover was on it! If it wasn't, I was going to have to look for it in the library on my own.

Next, he started our actual lesson talking about poems and how they were some of the oldest forms of storytelling. He told us they can be found in the Bible and pointed out how most of the books that were first read to us as children were really poems, just with pictures. Then he asked for a volunteer to read a poem aloud.

I raised my hand immediately, thinking, *Pick me! Pick me!* Seeing the hands of the other students, with their fingers all spread out, suddenly reminded me of Cammie at the meeting last night, counting off the words "you-did-it-to-me."

That's right, I thought as I lowered my hand. *I'm supposed to be treating Taylor like she's Jesus.* How quickly I'd forgotten all the things my sisters and I had spoken about the night before! I had asked them all for mom-like advice, and they had all told me to be kind to Taylor, and here I was, giving up so fast. Then it hit me why. What was the *first* thing my sisters all agreed that Mom would recommend I do? *Pray* about my problems. I hadn't really done that!

I'd better do it now. I waited until the student chosen to

95

read aloud began before I bowed my head and folded my hands together.

Dear Lord, being kind to people who aren't kind to you can be hard. Please help me to remember that you live in Taylor and in me so that I can treat her like you would. Amen—oh! One more thing. If Taylor really is hurting, like the way Kitty said she might be, then please show me how I can help her. Thank you! Amen for real this time!

When I opened my eyes, I felt both calmer and more determined. I not only wanted to follow God better, I believed that he was going to help me do so. It gave me a feeling of stillness that felt comforting, like when your mom or dad covers you with an extra blanket on a cold winter's night. *Keep speaking, Lord,* I thought. *I'll keep trying to listen.*

Chapter 12

When the change bell rang, I bolted out of the classroom before anyone else. I mean, I loved creative writing, but I also loved gym! On the first day of school I had even made sure to find out where the gymnasium was located, so I would know exactly where to go when the time came for me to have my first class.

Nikki, of course, felt the same way about gym as I did. We found each other outside the gymnasium, and after hesitating at the sight of one another, raced each other inside. Once we were in the locker room, we changed into our shorts and T-shirts, and were out on the gym floor in record time. Then we both ran toward a mat like it was the finish line in a marathon. We ended up reaching it at the same time and collapsing on top of it together, yelling, "It's a tie!" and laughing. Then, as we waited for our classmates to join us, we began practicing cartwheels and flips on the mat, with Nikki going over some of the choreography for the Gracelet routine with me.

Taylor and Krista had gym with us too. They came out of the locker room together a couple of minutes later and watched us. Neither of them said anything until I was in the middle of a cartwheel and Taylor shouted, "Break a leg!"

I clumsily fell out of my cartwheel.

I could hear Taylor snicker at me.

Krista's voice sounded a little shocked (but also like she was holding back a laugh, which I didn't like) when she said, "Taylor! You don't say that to gymnasts! You say that to actors before a play. It means 'good luck.' When you say that to a gymnast, it means, well, break a leg!"

"But I said, '*don't* break a leg.'" Taylor protested. She blinked hard in pretend surprise.

"I only heard 'break a leg'." Krista frowned with confusion.

"Oh, no." Taylor's smile was a smug little "u." "I just wanted Ansley—and Nikki—to be careful, that's all."

"That's nice," Krista said approvingly.

I shot a glance at Nikki to see what she thought. Nikki shook her head and shrugged, as if to say, "silly Taylor." She obviously didn't realize that Taylor had said what she had on purpose.

Soon, our gym teacher, Ms. Sharon, broke us up into groups and had us playing four games of volleyball in the four corners of the gym. I thought it was good that she separated us into teams, so no one had to feel bad about being picked last or anything like that. Unfortunately, when she divided us into teams, Taylor and I were on opposite sides of the net.

I was on the same team as Bethany, the girl Taylor had been whispering to in homeroom. I was glad that I had taken off my bow in the locker room (because I didn't want to get it all sweaty) so they couldn't be mean about it anymore. But I was not so glad to find Bethany on *my* team. *Is she going to be all fake-nice to me now because we're on the same side?* I wondered. *Or will she still be mean?* was surprised a few minutes later to find myself starting to feel sorry for her.

Bethany reminded me a lot of Damaris, one of my best friends at my old school. Damaris was great, but she was the opposite of me: she couldn't stand gym. She thought it was torture and was *not* sporty at all. She wasn't very coordinated or outdoorsy, either. But she was good at other things. She could do hard math in her head without having to write it down, for instance. She could also crochet well, and besides English, of course, could speak Spanish and Greek.

I was sure that, like Damaris, Bethany enjoyed doing other things. I just didn't know what those things were. What I did know was that she did *not* like gym. Her body language said it all: her shoulders were hunched up, her head was hanging down, and she kept scratching her arms every few minutes like she was being bitten by invisible mosquitoes. Most of all, whenever the ball came toward her, she would duck away from it instead of trying to hit it back over the net.

Our teammates started getting mad at her. They growled and grumbled under their breath, muttering not-so-nice things that I was sure she could hear.

She's not going to get any better at this game if her own team is against her, I thought. Then I remembered how encouraging the other gymnasts had been to me my first time at Grace-n-Power. Even the kids who were in other classes had called out encouragement to me.

The next time the ball came flying in Bethany's direction, I cheered, "You can do it, Beth!" And even though she *didn't* get it (in fact, she still kind of ran away from it) I patted her on the back. "You'll get the next one!" I said.

She looked at me with both doubt and hope in her eyes.

The next time the ball came toward her, she made a feeble attempt to hit it back over the net. The ball made light contact with one of her wrists, fell to the floor, and rolled away. Some of our teammates clucked their tongues in disappointment, but I jumped up and down for her. "See? Good try!" I pumped my fist in the air.

She flashed me a tiny smile.

At the end of the game, she even managed to hit one over the net. We didn't win, but I was so genuinely proud of her that I whooped and clapped my hands. "Great job, Beth!" This time she grinned with surprise at what she'd been able to do, as well as at our other teammates who had joined in cheering for her. It seemed that they all realized she had come a long way in just one game and were happy for her too.

When Ms. Sharon saw what was going on, she nodded at us and flashed a thumbs-up. "Love it! *Great* sportsmanship, you guys!"

As I wiped sweat from my forehead, I caught a glimpse of the winning team. They were all dancing around and cheering their victory—all except for Taylor, who stood with her hands on her hips, pouting. She looked strangely unhappy for someone on a team that had just won a game.

I discovered why after I changed back into my uniform and looked for a mirror to tie the bow back on my head. I was heading toward the girls' room when I heard the voices of Taylor and Bethany behind the next row of lockers. Hearing my name, I froze in place.

"Why were you nice to Ansley?" Taylor asked huffily. From the sound of her voice, I could even picture her sneering.

Bethany's voice was high and unsure. "Well, *she* was nice to *me*, really."

"I told you, she thinks she can do everything. 'Oh, look at me do gymnastics! Look at me, I can bake! Oh, yeah, and I know Mallory Winston too!' Ugh! She makes me sick!"

"Is it true she knows Mallory Winston, though? I heard about that. That's pretty cool."

Taylor sucked in her lips. "Please. I'll only believe it when I see it. Anyway, like I said, she's just a show-off, and the best way to deal with show-offs is to not pay any attention to them. Okay?"

"But . . . she wasn't a show-off during the game," Bethany said. "She didn't hog the ball or try to score all the points or anything like that."

"But she was still a show-off," Taylor insisted. "She was try-ing to get all the attention by being the nicest and most . . . sportsmanlike."

An uncomfortable silence fell between them. I could even feel the tension from where I stood.

Then Bethany spoke again, "But Krista seems to like her. And Krista is your best friend."

"You mean *was* my best friend. Now all she seems to talk about these days is Ansley, Ansley, Ansley. I wish she'd never moved in next door to Krista."

Again, awkward silence fell between them. Finally, Bethany piped up, "But . . . didn't you tell me that you invited Ansley to your bakery party on Friday?"

"Yeah, but only because I *had* to. She's going to ruin everything."

"Ruin it?" I heard a locker door slam closed. "How's she going to do that?"

"I don't know. She just will. You'll see." Another locker door slammed. "Come on, we'd better go before we're late to class."

I made sure to duck out of sight as Taylor and Bethany left the locker room. Once I was sure they were both gone, I leaned against a tiled wall in shock. I knew that Taylor disliked me, I just hadn't known how much. *How was I ever going to get her to change her mind about me?*

Chapter 13

I acted cheerful the rest of the afternoon at school, but I couldn't pretend with my family afterwards. That evening, as we all sat together at the dinner table, I shoved my mashed potatoes around my plate as my sisters chattered about their day. I was too lost in my thoughts to pay attention to what they were saying. It was my father's voice that cut through my fog.

"Ansley? Ansley, what's wrong?"

"What?" I looked up at him sort of dazed. "What do you mean? Nothing's wrong." I didn't mean to lie. I just didn't want to worry him.

"Oh, yes there is!" my sisters all chorused.

My father tilted his head at them. "You can't fool us. When the chattiest Daniels sister is the quietest, she's either sick or something else is wrong. And you don't look like you have a fever." His voice was gentle and kind. "Why don't you tell us what's bothering you?"

I let out a deep breath. "Okay. I mean, the girls pretty much know about this already." I looked over at all of them. "But it's only gotten worse today." And I told them all about my troubles with Taylor.

My father and aunt listened without interrupting me. I told them everything, beginning with the insult about the bow I had been wearing to the conversation that I had heard between Taylor and Bethany in the locker room.

"Well, at least you know now why she doesn't like you," Aunt Sam said when I was done.

"I do? Why?"

"She's jealous of you."

"Is *that* it?"

"Yes, and jealousy can be a very powerful emotion. She feels like you have so much going for you—talent, personality, goodness—and sees how attracted other people are to it. She's even afraid that you're stealing her best friend."

"But I'm not. I mean, I don't have a best friend yet. I just have a lot of friends. I like hanging around a lot of people and having friends. I'm not doing anything wrong—and I'm not showing off! Oh, except that one time . . ."

And I told them all about the Mallory Winston incident. When I was done, the twins exchanged glances and smiled, and even Dad was smiling a little.

"Did I say something funny?"

My father's face got serious again. "No, honey. In fact, I think it's good that you realized you were boasting and that it was wrong. After all, we should only boast in the Lord or not at all."

"How can we 'boast in the Lord?'" Kitty asked.

"It means to boast about God's goodness, not our own. Any good that we do is through God's grace in us, anyway."

"Like my being able to do gymnastics or bake really well. They are gifts God gave to me. I'm only using them like I'm supposed to," I said with new understanding. "So how can I make her not jealous? How can I make Taylor like me?"

Dad reached across the table and covered one of my hands with his. "You can't," he said.

"Huh?"

"You can't *make* a person like you. You can only—and *should* only—be yourself. If other people like you when you're yourself, then that's great. But you shouldn't have to perform tricks or favors or change who you are to get people to like you.

"I think the advice your sisters gave you—to pray about the situation, to be kind to Taylor, to consider that she might be hurting inside—was all excellent advice, and I'm proud of them for giving it to you. To add to what they said, though, I'm going to remind you of something Jesus said that is written in the book of Matthew, chapter five—"

I jumped up from my chair. "Oh, wait! Let me look it up in my new Bible!" I ran for my knapsack as my family waited patiently for my return.

When I did, my sisters surrounded me as I flipped over to the Gospel of Matthew.

"There's chapter five," Lena pointed.

"What verse? What verse?" Kitty asked.

"Forty-four. Make that forty-three and forty-four."

We ran our hands over the fine print.

"Found them! Found them!" Cammie sang out.

"Let me read it, please," I said, clearing my throat and holding the Bible out in front of me. "You have heard that it was said, 'Love your neighbor and hate your enemy.' But I tell you, love your enemies and pray for those who persecute you . . ." I looked up from the page. "Oh."

"Something clicked for you, didn't it?" my father said. "What was the 'oh' for?"

I slowly put the Bible down on the table. "Only that, well, I prayed for God to help me, and I prayed to God to show *me* how to help her, but I didn't exactly pray *for* Taylor directly."

"Good, good. You're understanding. That's a gift from the Holy Spirit, by the way—understanding. Now turn to the book of Luke."

"Let me! Let me!" Kitty and Cammie both stretched out their hands.

"Only if you're careful!" I admonished them. "This Bible is new! We're supposed to take extra good care of it!"

"I'll have you both read something, so you can each have a turn," Dad said. "So carefully take the Bible, Cammie, and turn to the book of Luke, chapter six, verses twenty-seven and twenty-eight."

Cammie gently took the Bible from me and reverently turned the pages to the right place. Then she read, "But to you who are listening I say: Love your enemies, do good to those who hate you, bless those who curse you, pray for those who mistreat you." She looked up. "Isn't that the same thing as before?"

Dad, who had taken his own Bible out of his bag and was reading along with her, said, "Now read verse thirty-one."

"'Do to others as you would have them do to you.' Oh! The Golden Rule!"

"Right."

"So I have to keep treating Taylor the way I'd like her to treat me," I said, "even if she keeps being mean? That's not going to be easy."

"Well, you can't be *mean* to her," Lena said. "That's not what Jesus would do."

"I didn't say I'd be mean to her," I said. "Just that it's going to be hard to be nice to her if she keeps this up."

"Can't I read something?" Kitty asked Dad.

"Of course. Hand her the Bible, Cam. Kitty, continue where Cammie left off. Read verses thirty-two and thirty-three."

"All righty," Kitty said. "'If you love those who love you, what credit is that to you? Even sinners love those who love them. And if you do good to those who are good to you, what credit is that to you? Even sinners do that.'" She looked at Dad expectantly.

"Loving each other is what makes us Christians. Even when people make it harder to love them sometimes," Dad said. "Lena, why don't you finish? Read verse thirty-five."

Lena stood up straight and read clearly, "But love your enemies, do good to them, and lend to them without expecting to get anything back."

"And that's key," my dad said as Lena closed the Bible. "As a follower of Jesus, you are called to show her love and mercy. *But* you can't expect her to show you love and mercy back. You can't give to get."

I summed it up. "You mean I'm supposed to be kind to her because it's the right thing to do."

"Exactly."

I nodded without saying anything. It looked like I had some work to do.

"Anyway," Dad said as a smile spread across his face. "It was funny your mentioning Mallory Winston earlier, Ansley, because . . ."

Dad's phone went off.

"Perfect timing," he said, holding up the phone. "She's calling us right now."

Chapter 14

"She's FaceTiming us!" I said, feeling slightly panicked. I had just admitted to my entire family that I'd boasted about knowing Mallory Winston, and now all I wanted to do was duck under the table. I was so embarrassed.

"Hi, Mallory!" Dad said after her big hair and smiling face appeared on his phone screen.

"Hi, Daniels family!" Mallory's friendly voice rang out. She waved to all of us. Dad turned his phone so that the camera could pan the table showing her that we were all there, waving back. I bowed my head. I just couldn't look her in the face.

My sisters all leapt to their feet to crowd around Dad's phone. I got to my feet, too, but to help Aunt Sam clear the table.

"How are you all doing?" Mallory asked. "I'm sorry I haven't been in touch lately. Y'all know how sorry I am about Mrs. Daniels' passing. I was always so impressed with her when I watched her with you girls. And she was such a prayerful woman. She was always a real blessing to have around."

"Yes, she was," Dad said. "Thank you for saying it." The rest of us nodded in silent agreement.

"I actually have a special reason for calling that kind of has to do with your mother," Mallory said. "When I'd heard she'd gone to the Lord, it got me thinking a lot about what our faith is all about. I felt your loss real heavy, but I also felt the powerful faith of your family that she's with Jesus and that you will all see one another again one day.

"After praying for all of you I felt moved to write a song for y'all, and if you like it and let me, I'd like to put it on my next album."

"Wow!"

"Really?"

"That's amazing!"

As my family crowded around the phone and exclaimed over Mallory's exciting news, I found myself drawn to join them. So I tiptoed over and craned my neck over Kitty's shoulder to get a look at Mallory.

"Can I play it for you right now?" she asked. "Then you can let me know what you think." After everyone enthusiastically agreed, she placed her phone on a shelf of some kind and then backed away from it as it continued recording. Then she sat down on a chair, picked up a guitar, and began to sing:

> *We'll meet again*
> *At the happy reunion,*
> *Where we'll be singing songs of praise,*
> *Standing in the light of heaven*
> *And His all-loving gaze.*
> *We'll remember not our sadness*
> *In the joy of that embrace.*
> *Our only tears will be of gladness*
> *For His forgiveness and His grace . . .*

As Mallory continued, I felt as if her song lifted my soul to a happy, hopeful place. And when she was finished, I was feeling so good that I found it easy to look at her again without feeling embarrassed, although to see her *clearly* I had to blink back a few tears.

Dad found his voice first. "That was just beautiful, Mallory. A lovely tribute to Mrs. Daniels and a wonderful song of hope and faith."

"I'm so glad you liked it. I was thinking if it's all right with you, I'd like to release it as the first single off my new album. I'll not only dedicate the song to your mother, Lena, but I'll donate all the proceeds to charity. Did she have any favorite causes?"

"She didn't have a favorite charity," Dad said, "but she did give to quite a few. I'll do a little research and talk it over with the girls. We'll figure out the best place for your donation to go. Thanks so much, Mallory. It always made their mother so happy to be able to help others. She would be thrilled to know she is still able to do something for her fellow man even now."

"I'm sure she *does* know," Mallory said softly. Then she clasped her hands together. "Now that I have the Daniels family stamp of approval, I would like to debut this song in a live surprise appearance at the Roland Lake Founder's Day Fair. How does that sound?"

"That sounds great!" Lena said. As the rest of us chimed in that we thought so, too, Lena's eyes were shining. "Actually, Mallory, we'll be performing one of your songs there—I mean, my church high school choir will."

"That's not the only time you'll be singing at the fair if I get my way." Mallory smiled mischievously.

"Huh?" Lena asked. "What do you mean?"

"I mean would you consider singing "Happy Reunion" at the fair with me?"

Lena looked stunned. *"What?"*

"You know, as a duet. I can send you a recording of the song with harmonies to practice along with."

"But—but—how do you know I'd even be good enough?" Lena sputtered.

"Because I've heard you sing, Lena, and you sound phenomenal! We need to get you out there so people can hear how good you are!"

Lena placed a hand on her head as if to keep it from floating off her neck. "I don't understand! When have you heard me sing?"

Mallory smiled with amusement. "This morning when I received a video of you singing and playing the guitar. I didn't know you were a songwriter too! I think we definitely need to work together."

"Dad! I can't believe you did that!" Lena turned to Dad in accusation. She didn't seem to know whether to be happy or angry about it.

"I didn't do it!" Dad raised his hands up in surrender. "Your sisters did."

"Huh? I didn't do anything!" I said, copying Dad and raising my hands in surrender.

"No, it was the twins," Dad clarified. "When they emailed your grandmothers this morning, they sent them a video of you singing the other night, and then they asked if they could send a video to Mallory as well. I said they could."

Lena stood in dazed amazement.

"So . . ." Mallory's voice coming out of the phone brought Lena back to reality. "What do you say? Will you sing with me?"

"How can I say no? Especially for such a special song," Lena said. "So . . . yes, of course I'll sing with you."

"You've made me so happy, Lena. God seems to still have plans for us to work together for His purpose. I believe that this song will bring God's comfort to other people who are also going through a difficult time. And we can make sure that any money it makes can also go to help people in need. I'm so glad our partnership isn't over. I'll send you the music file in a few minutes."

After receiving the file, Lena went to her room to listen to it and to start practicing her part of the duet. Dad went to his office to do a little work, and I went to the upstairs family room with the twins and Aunt Sam.

Cammie and Kitty went straight back to working on the "Winter's Paradise" puzzle since they hadn't finished it the other day, while I looked over paperwork for the Bake Off with Aunt Sam.

She curled up on the white couch and scanned the info sheet as Zette hopped up next to her and snuggled against her leg. "Okay, it says here that there will be three baking challenges. The first two will be held on Saturday and the big one is on Sunday.

"The first kids' challenge is a pastry of your choosing that falls under the category of 'My Specialty,'" she read aloud from the sheet. "This should be a pastry that you are well known for, is a family favorite, or can even be called your signature dish."

I turned to smile at Kitty and Cam just as they turned to me with smiles of their own. "Cinnamon rolls!" we said at the same time.

"The second challenge," Aunt Sam continued, "is the cookies or bars challenge. It falls under the category of 'With a Twist.'"

I wrinkled my nose. "What's that supposed to mean?"

Again, Aunt Sam read from the printout. "Whether it is brownies or lemon bars, ginger snaps or sugar cookies, baked in a pan or on a sheet, present us with a familiar, delish dessert in a fresh, new way. Add an unexpected flavor, change its typical appearance, or otherwise surprise us with your originality."

"Hmm." It sounded to me like the second challenge was going to take a little more thought. "I guess I can do my blondies but add something a little different to them."

Cam made a face. "I like your blondies the way they are. Why change them?"

"To meet the requirements of the challenge," I pointed out.

"Just don't add anything weird to them," Kitty said. She stuck out her tongue and shuddered. "Like cayenne pepper or pickles or something."

I slapped my forehead. "I won't! Okay, Aunt Sam, what about Sunday?"

"That's when things get really interesting. That's the day the winners of ribbons in the first two challenges bake *on premises* for a chance at the Grand Prize. It says here that there will be ovens set up under the tents and that the TV show *Awake with the Lake* will be filming."

"I have a question," I said. "If we aren't baking there on Saturday, I guess that means we have to bring in our dishes, right?"

"Yes."

"So how can they be sure you really made the desserts you're bringing in on Saturday?"

"Actually, I was just getting to that. It says here that you're supposed to film yourself making those dishes." Aunt Sam put a hand on her hip and smiled down at the twins. "I wonder if we'll be able to fulfill that rule. You don't happen to know any-one who's good at recording stuff, do you?"

Kitty and Cam chuckled in a way that seemed to say "guilty as charged" as well as "and proud of it!"

"And what's the Cake Challenge theme again?" I asked, reaching for the printout.

"Don't you remember?" Aunt Sam handed me the sheet. "Favorite of the Fair."

"Oh, right. So basically, that means I'll just have to bake a cake *everybody* likes. That's all. No pressure or anything." Now I was starting to feel a little nervous. "Any ideas?" I nudged Kitty with my big toe.

"Maybe if you made something chocolate? People usually like chocolate."

"Not everyone does, though," I reminded her. "I usually pre-fer vanilla. So does Cam. Chocolate's not my favorite thing in the world—unless it's Aunt Sam's awesome chocolate cake!" I sat up with a bolt. "Hey! What about you, Aunt Sam? What will *you* be entering in the fair?"

"Oh, I decided against entering this year," Aunt Sam admit-ted, to my surprise. "I won't have time to be involved in all that when I need to be looking after you girls. But maybe next year."

"That's too bad." I felt genuinely sad for all the people who weren't going to get the chance to eat her cake at the fair.

"But maybe you can make your Famous Perfect Chocolate Cake for *us*?" Kitty, who was sitting cross-legged on the rug as she worked on the puzzle, looked up at Aunt Sam and blinked big, begging eyes.

"You look more like a puppy-dog than a kitty cat," Aunt Sam

said with a laugh. "But sure. One of these days I'll make it for you girls."

"Sooooon?" Cam curled up her hands to look like a dog's front paws and began panting at Aunt Sam's knees. Zette lifted her head from Aunt Sam's lap to give Cam a perplexed look before settling back down again.

Aunt Sam chuckled as she stroked Zette's head. "I think we're going to be up to our ears in baked goods around here—at least for a while—but yes, I'll make it soon."

"Yesss!" I high-fived with my sisters.

I looked over the sheet again and found myself suddenly getting anxious. "Wait, so I have to bring in *two* desserts in one day?"

"There are two challenges on Saturday. One in the morning and one in the afternoon," Aunt Sam said. "But you don't *have* to enter both categories, you know."

Entering both challenges would mean a lot of baking on the night before. That meant Friday! The day of Taylor's baking party! "Maybe I shouldn't go to the party . . ."

Aunt Sam shook her head. "You already said 'yes' to that. It would be impolite to back out now."

I sank back against the sofa cushions. "She doesn't even want me there."

"But your other friends do," Cammie said as she neatly pressed a puzzle piece into the puzzle. It fit perfectly.

"Maybe," Kitty tilted her head thoughtfully, "you can make something at the party you can enter into the Bake Off."

"That would be great! But I doubt that'll happen. At least the visit there might inspire me with some ideas, anyway," I said. "And what about the Grace-n-Power performance? *When* is that supposed to be?"

"Sunday afternoon—a little before Lena's choir performs. And from what Mallory told us before she hung up, her surprise appearance will be right after that. Hopefully her duet with Lena won't run into the time of the Favorite Cake of the Fair judging."

"Why? When is that?"

"Well, let's see. According to the rules of the Bake Off, if you get a ribbon in one of the previous challenges and qualify for the third challenge, you have to check in by eight-thirty in the morning to claim your spot. Baking starts by nine. You get two hours. Presentation is at eleven. Then fairgoers are invited to the tents to taste all the entries. The winner will be announced by three o'clock."

"I really don't want to miss Mallory and Lena's performance," I said. "But I guess I shouldn't worry about that unless I get a ribbon in one of the first two challenges, anyway."

"It sounds kind of funny to *worry* about *winning*," Cammie pointed out.

I chuckled. "You're right!" But I found myself worrying anyway. *What if I win the Bake Off but missed the duet? That would be terrible!* I shook my head. *That wouldn't happen.* Awake with the Lake *wouldn't want to miss Mallory Winston, either.*

I was sure of it.

Chapter 15

On Thursday morning I stared down at the pink and purple headscarf I held in my hand and took a deep breath. *Do I wear it, or don't I? I asked myself. Do I let Taylor make me feel bad about something that isn't bad? Something that used to make me feel happy? Do I let her control how I want to style myself? Or do I put the bow on and take a chance on her making fun of me again—possibly all day long and to other people?*

Suddenly I jumped at the sound of someone knocking on my door. It was weird to hear since I was the one who usually did the knocking early in the morning. Then I heard, "Are you ready yet? Come on! It's time for breakfast!" It was Cammie.

"I'll be right there!" I yelled through the closed door. "I just need to do one last thing!" And, pressing my lips together, I determinedly tied the bow into my hair before joining my sisters downstairs.

Once I got to the kitchen table, I noticed all my sisters sitting on one side of the table, with Cammie holding up a phone, recording my entrance into the kitchen. Then I noticed something else: all three of my sisters were wearing hair bows too. I gasped.

Lena grinned. "After hearing what happened yesterday, we decided we weren't going to let you face Taylor alone."

"I hope you don't mind us copying you," Kitty said, looking up at me with serious eyes.

My heart felt warm and soft. "No, I don't mind. I don't mind at all. This is so cool of you guys. Thank you!"

"Together *four*-ever!" Lena started to chant.

"Together *four*-ever!" The rest of us joined in. "Together *four*-ever! Together *four*-eveeeeerrrr!"

Once we were dropped off at school and the twins dashed off to meet their friends, Lena gestured for me to follow her under the shade of a nearby tree and away from running, laughing, and chattering students.

"I've been wanting to thank you again for praying with me the other night," she said in a low voice, since our conversation was private. "You must have some powerful faith. Look what's happened since then! I'm going to be singing with Mallory Winston! On stage! In front of an audience and everything!" She got a faraway look in her eye for a minute before returning to the present moment. "Anyway, I wanted to return the favor and pray with you. Especially about this Taylor situation. Would you like to?"

"Sure!" I put out my hands so that she could take them in hers.

Lena closed her eyes. "Dear God, thank you so much for hearing my sister Ansley's prayer for me and for showing me the path you'd like me to follow. I am so grateful for your love and guidance. Now Ansley and I come together again to pray for someone else.

"We pray for Taylor because she is a child of yours that you love very much. We don't know if she is going through any struggles right now, but if she is, we pray that you send her the strength she needs to handle them and the comfort she needs to deal with them. We also ask that you please use Ansley as an instrument to help Taylor and to remind Taylor that you love her. We also ask, Lord, that you please soften Taylor's heart so that it can be more like yours and she can be kinder to my sister. We praise you and thank you for all your blessings. Amen."

When she was done, we let go of one another's hands and fell into a hug.

"Thanks, Lena," I said, my chin resting on her shoulder.

"Anytime, Sis."

As we both headed toward school, we noticed something a little strange: a number of girls seemed to be wearing bows in their hair just like us. I felt like I must be imagining it, but when I turned to Lena I could see her scanning the crowd with a quizzical expression on her face.

"Do you see what I see?" she asked me.

"Yeah . . . all the hair bows?"

"Yeah."

"Did you tell other people to wear them too?"

"No," Lena said. "I promise I didn't. That's why I'm surprised to see—" She stopped speaking because at that moment Krista ran over to us—and she was wearing a pink, sparkly scarf as a bow.

"Hi, Ansley! Oh, hi, Lena!"

"Hi," I said. "I . . . like your bow."

Krista flushed red. "Thanks. I just liked yours so much yesterday that I wanted to try the look for myself. So, I, uh, kinda copied you."

"It looks really nice," I told her truthfully.

Krista gestured at the kids on the grounds. "Obviously I wasn't the only one who liked your bow yesterday."

I could see by Lena's face that a thought was occurring to her. "You know what, Ansley?" she began to laugh. "I think you started a trend!"

"What?"

Krista nodded as we all looked around at the seemingly growing number of girls milling about the entrance to the middle school who were wearing bows made of scarves in their hair.

Lena pointed to her own head. "It's even hit the high school." She winked at me. "Gotta run. Have a great day at school, you guys!"

"Thanks, you too, Lena!" We waved as she dashed away from us.

"Oh, look, here comes Taylor," Krista said. "She didn't get bit by the bow bug, I see."

I smiled to myself. I hadn't expected her to!

"Hi, Taylor!" Krista grinned at her straight-faced friend. "What, you didn't get the memo?" she joked. "We're all wearing head scarves now."

Taylor stopped in her tracks. "Well, *I'm* not."

Krista looked a little deflated at Taylor's lack of enthusiasm, but I was feeling so lighthearted to see so many other girls wearing bows that Taylor's attitude didn't bother me at all.

Then I suddenly had a flash of insight that Taylor might be feeling like she wasn't cool because she *wasn't* wearing a bow. This made me feel a little bad for her, which surprised me, so I said, "Taylor doesn't need to wear a bow. She has a style all her own." And I gave her a genuine smile.

Instead of smiling back, Taylor just stared at me. Then the school bell rang.

"Time to go in!" I said. And I practically skipped as I led them inside the front doors.

Taylor didn't say a word about my head scarf all homeroom long. And when the bell rang, we went our separate ways since I was taking Spanish while she was taking French, so I didn't have to see her until lunch time.

Only I didn't see her at lunch time, because she didn't show up.

"Where did Taylor go?" I asked, taking my peanut butter and jelly sandwich out of my bag.

"Beats me," Guadalupe said.

"She had to go to the doctor," Krista said, "so her grandma picked her up."

Guadalupe clutched her cross pendant. "The *doctor*?"

"Why?" Nikki asked.

"Is she sick?" I squeaked.

"No, not that kind of doctor." Krista scooped up a sporkful of the tuna salad she had purchased in the cafeteria. "The kind you talk to about your feelings." She dropped her spork and covered her mouth. "Ooh. I wasn't supposed to say anything. Please don't let her know I told you guys."

"You mean like a counselor?" I asked. My sisters and I went to one to talk about our feelings about our mom.

"Yeah. But Taylor doesn't like to talk about it," Krista said.

"Oh." So my sisters were right. There *was* something bothering Taylor.

The table got a little quiet. Then Nikki said in a soft voice, "That's why my dad always says that we should always choose to be kind toward others because 'everyone is fighting a battle you know nothing about.'"

"I don't understand," Guadalupe said. "What do you mean, 'battle?' Who is Taylor fighting?"

"It's not 'who,' necessarily, it's 'what,'" Nikki said. And she reminded me a little bit of her preacher father when she explained, "It means that everyone has their share of suffering. You know, bad things in their lives that they have to get through. Things they might not be telling other people about. They could be battling against sadness, or anger, or a situation in their lives that's hard or scary. And since all people suffer, we should try to remember that and help each other out. To help make each other's lives better instead of worse."

"You mean love your neighbor," I said, then added under my breath, "and your enemies."

"Exactly." Nikki nodded.

"Then let's all try to be more kind to Taylor," Krista announced.

"Yes, let's!"

"Good idea!"

"Kindness helps," I said, thinking about all the ways people had been kind to me and my family after my mother died. "It really helps a lot."

After school, I went to Grace-n-Power with Guadalupe and Nikki and practiced my two tumbling passes for the Gracelet performance. We kept them short and simple since there was no time to work on something fancy. Plus, Coach Flip didn't want me doing anything too complicated or that wouldn't go well with the choreography of the routine. In the end, it was only a few seconds of stage time in a routine that was only about three minutes long anyway. We just wanted to make those seconds count.

When we were back in the locker room changing, I heard both Nikki and Guadalupe humming the Mallory Winston song we had used in the routine and I blurted, "You wanna know something really cool? Mal—" Then I snapped my mouth shut.

I didn't want to tell them that Mallory Winston had called my house. That she had played a new song for us—a song she had written especially for my mom. I would sound like a show-off again. Plus, Mallory's appearance at the fair was supposed to be a surprise.

Guadalupe and Nikki blinked at me, waiting.

"Well?" Nikki asked finally.

"Never mind," I said. "It's something about my sister and the fair this weekend, but—"

"I know what you were going to say," Nikki said with a knowing smile.

"You do?" I was shocked. How could she know?

"Yes." Nikki undid her bun and changed it into a high pony-tail. "You heard us humming that Mallory song and it made you remember that the high school choir is going to sing a Mallory Winston song at the fair, didn't you?"

She was kind of right, actually. So I just nodded silently.

"And your big sister's in the choir, isn't she? I think they are supposed to perform right after we do. So we'll have back-to-back Mallory Winston songs—not to mention back-to-back performances by the Daniels sisters. Is that what you were going to say?"

"Something like that, yes."

"But you didn't want to sound like you were boasting again."

Nikki was sure she had it all figured out. "Don't worry. It's totally okay to be excited about the performances. And we don't mind if you talk about Mallory Winston, do we, Guadalupe?"

"It's fine," Guadalupe agreed.

"Thanks, guys." I said. I was grateful to have such understanding friends. "So, after our performance, can you guys stay with me to hear the choir sing?"

"Sure," Guadalupe said. She zipped up her duffel bag and slung it on her shoulder.

"Of course!" Nikki agreed.

"Great. I'd like for both of you to hear Lena sing. She's really good." I led the way out of the locker room, proud of myself for not giving away Mallory's surprise. "And I think her performance will be something you won't want to miss."

Chapter 16

On Friday, Taylor was back in school and back to her old tricks. Or at least she tried to be. But when Bethany came to homeroom wearing a yellow head scarf tied in a bow, Taylor seemed to decide against whispering to her about me behind my back. Instead, she resorted to either ignoring me or glaring at me.

I actually preferred the ignoring to the glaring. All during homeroom, I felt like she was shooting lasers at me with her eyes, and I kept rubbing the back of my head. I especially felt the "burn" when she overheard Krista telling me how her grandmother, Hunni, would be driving the two of us to her baking party at Lynda's Lovin' Oven later that afternoon. She seemed to soften, though, when Krista added, "Wait til you see the place! It's the cutest bakery ever!" And I had to admit that I really was looking forward to going despite Taylor's behavior.

After lunch, it was prayer journal time. Ms. J-J put some music on real low and reminded us to write about the one time in the week we felt closest to God and the one time we felt furthest away. When I opened my journal and saw the words, "Speak, Lord, for your servant is listening," it made me stop, close my eyes, and ask God for help.

Remembering the time I felt furthest away was easy. It was when I had acted boastful about Mallory, so I wrote about that. But when I felt closest was harder because I had so many times to choose from: making my sisters happy with the after-school snack surprise, my sisters all trying to help me with their advice, praying with Lena both times. There was a lot of love in my family, and where there was love, there was God.

Then it struck me. The time I felt closest to God this week was when I first heard Mallory's song "Happy Reunion." It had made me feel closer to my family as we listened to it together, closer to my mom in heaven since it was about seeing her again, and closer to God, because it made me feel washed clean about boasting since it was Mallory who had called and sang it to us. It had lifted my soul. *That,* I thought with a nod as I bent over my journal, *is definitely the moment to write about.*

And when I did, I felt like my soul was uplifted again! It was a good feeling.

When I was done, there was still some time left. I was looking around the room absentmindedly when my eyes fell upon Taylor, scribbling in her book. I was surprised to feel a pang in my heart at the sight of her. I turned back to my journal.

Dear God, I wrote. *Please let Taylor have a good time at her party today. Please don't let her think I've 'ruined' it by coming. Just let her have some fun. I think she could use it. Amen.*

It was raining when Hunni picked us up after school, and the windshield wipers of her car squeaked the whole drive over. Luckily, the rain wasn't too hard, and the ride wasn't too long. And when Hunni pulled up beside a storefront with a pink and white striped awning, I didn't need her to say "Here we are!" to know that we had arrived.

After Krista and I scrambled out of the car and said goodbye to Hunni, we took a moment under the awning to smooth ourselves down and get a better look at the place. The bricks of the

building were painted in creamy white. The window displays were stocked with pink trays of neatly arranged frosted cupcakes and shiny breads so fresh that you could smell them from the street. And the logo in the window was a cartoon drawing of a sweetly smiling stove with hearts for cheeks that was rubbing its oven-belly and licking its lips (not that it really had any).

I followed Krista through the front door, and a little bell chimed to announce our arrival. The inside of the store was painted a ballerina pink, and the walls were dotted with gold-framed chalkboards that listed all the pastries and their prices in white or pink chalk. The glass display cases were stocked with goodies, and a girl behind the counter was sliding a new batch of cookies into it. The chocolate chips in them still looked warm and slightly gooey.

"Everything is so cute!" I squealed. *Maybe one day I'll open a bakery of my own,* I thought, inhaling the competing scents of sugar, vanilla, and butter. *After I've retired from gymnastics, of course. But what would I call it?* And I imagined a logo of a girl walking a balance beam while holding a loaf of bread in one hand and a multi-layered cake in the other. *The Balanced Bakery? Cakewalk?*

There were people sitting on white chairs arranged around small pink tables, drinking tea from rose-patterned cups, and eating dainty cakes from matching plates. A girl in an apron that matched the awning outside directed us toward a curtain near the back of the store. "You'll want to go that way. There's a private room."

Behind the curtain was a room with a dining area furnished with mini picnic tables painted in white. A mural depicting a parade of happy, smiling cupcakes, croissants, eclairs, layered cakes, and milkshakes decorated the longest wall. Next to it was a white kitchen that bustled with workers. "This is cool," I said.

Taylor was standing behind a counter in the kitchen area, scanning the girls seated at the tables with a concerned look on her face. I noticed she was wearing a pink and blue scarf around her head, tied in a bow. My mouth dropped open. She looked really cute, actually, but I could still barely believe it.

She spotted us and smiled. I shut my mouth to smile back, but as usual she wasn't really looking at me. She was looking at Krista, whom she ran over to, grabbed by the hand, and dragged back to the kitchen area with her. I shrugged to myself, found Nikki and Guadalupe at one of the tables, and sat down with them. Then, to my surprise, Bethany sat down next to me. She smiled at me, and I smiled back.

An older woman with short, styled red hair and wearing an apron that said, "Cookies make everything better" came out from the kitchen and greeted all of us. "Hi! Most of you already know me, but for those of you who don't, I'm Lynda, Taylor's grandma, and the owner of Lynda's Lovin' Oven! Welcome to my bakery and to Taylor's Back-to-School bakery party. Taylor, why don't you tell the girls what we'll be doing today?"

Taylor's face turned red and she looked down at her shoes for a moment. Then, after clearing her throat, she said in a voice so low that it was hard to hear her, "Thank you for coming, everyone. We're going to have lots of fun, um, baking cookies and decorating cakes." She walked to the first mini picnic table and her voice got a little louder, "This is the Mixing Station. This is where we will mix up and spoon out Grandma's Famous Super Dough. It works for all kinds of cookie recipes." She stepped over to my table. "This will be the Creative Station. As you can see, there are all sorts of things to mix into the cookie dough: chocolate chips, sprinkles, peanut butter, marshmallows, caramel, white chocolate, and so on.

"This next table is the Decorating Station." It was obvious that it was Taylor's favorite station, since her voice got louder and more excited. "This will be for decorating cakes we've already made." Taylor pointed to the kitchen counter behind her. "With frosting, marzipan, white chocolate, or my favorite, fondant.

"And then we'll clear all of the stations and eat all the goodies!"

Guadalupe got up from her seat. "I'm going to move to the Decorating Station. There's no wheat in most frosting or fondant and stuff, so it'll be better for me."

Taylor's grandma said, "You do that, honey. I've got gloves for you too." Then she clapped her hands. "So let's begin!"

We were all given aprons and chef hats made of some kind of recycled fabric, which I thought was both cool and fun. And even though I thought about joining the Mixing Station since I love the whole process of baking from scratch, I knew I would have to do that at home later for the Bake Off. So instead I decided to stay at the Creative Station. I thought it would be fun to randomly choose different things to mix into the cookie dough, like chocolate chips in this cookie, marshmallows in that one, hazelnut spread in the next. Sometimes I mixed two or three ingredients into a cookie at a time—like chocolate sprinkles and peanut butter—and hoped to be inspired with an idea for my blondies. *What can I put into my blondies that will make them different? Unexpected? Original? Yet still yummy?* I wondered.

I asked Bethany if she had any ideas.

"Oh, you're going to enter the Bake Off?" she asked. She seemed a little startled. "So's Taylor."

"Oh, right," I said, trying to act like I wasn't bothered by the news. I really wasn't surprised, but I was annoyed at myself for not thinking of it before. Of course, she was entering the Bake Off! I wondered if she was entering the second challenge.

"Maybe you can put peanut butter in the blondies," Bethany suggested, gesturing at the jar we had on the table. "Maybe the crunchy kind. That might be cool."

"It sounds delicious," I admitted. "But I don't think that's really a surprising ingredient."

"It does sound good, though," Nikki said, holding her stomach. "I wish we were making those right now." And we all laughed.

When I felt I had filled enough cookies and wanted to give someone else a turn, I wandered over to the Decorating Station. Guadalupe was rolling out fondant with a rolling pin and cutting shapes out of it with a cookie cutter. The girl next to her, Stella, was placing them on top of a chocolate cake. They were making a pretty design of big blue stars and small yellow ones on top of what looked like a background of white fondant covering an entire cake. Another pair of girls was piping pink rosettes made of frosting onto another cake. Two other girls were covering red velvet cupcakes with cream cheese frosting.

Taylor, however, was in her own world. She was sculpting little panda bears out of fondant. They weren't just pandas, they were baby pandas, in different poses that looked too adorable to eat. "Wow!" I said, unable to stop myself. "Those are amazing! And super cute!"

"Aren't they?" Krista, who was sitting next to her, piped up.

"Thanks," Taylor said, but I felt like she was eyeing me suspiciously.

"I wish I could do that," I said, sitting down.

"You mean you can't?" Taylor perked up a little.

"No way," I admitted freely. "If I could, I would make a unicorn and put it on top of a cake to make it a unicorn cake!"

"You and your unicorns," Taylor said, shaking her head. But she smiled a little.

"What are you making, Krista?" I could see her rolling white balls in different sizes and stacking them on top of one another. "Are those snowmen?"

She laughed at herself. "Basically, this is the best I can do! So, yeah. Snowmen!"

Then, feeling a shadow looming over me, I turned around to see Lynda standing behind me. "You must be Ansley, the new girl," she said. With her lipstick a shade of pink that matched the store, her smile was picture-perfect. But I couldn't help feeling like she was sizing me up.

"Yes, ma'am."

"I hear you're quite the little baker."

"Yes, I love to bake," I said.

She puffed up her chest. "Taylor's entering the Bake Off tomorrow."

I nodded. "Yes, ma'am. So am I, ma'am."

Lynda exhaled. Taylor stopped what she was doing. "You are?" they both asked at the same time.

I nodded.

"Well, isn't that nice," Lynda said. "Best of luck to you, then, sweetheart." She pointed to the pandas. "You'll need it."

I raised my eyebrows at that remark but said nothing.

Lynda addressed the group. "Okay, everyone," she said, clapping her hands again. I had the feeling she had once been a teacher. "It's time to put the cookies in the oven and taste some of these beautifully decorated creations! But first let's take some pictures of all the work you did so you can remember what they looked like before they got eaten."

As the girls posed proudly with their cakes, I slipped away and joined Guadalupe again. "What are you going to eat?" I asked her.

"Rice squares," she told me. "They have that and flan here for people like me."

"But no gluten-free cake?"

"No. Even if they wanted to, they would have to bake the cake in a pan that had not been used for regular cakes with gluten, and it couldn't be cooked in an oven that had anything with gluten in it, so . . ." Guadalupe shrugged and slid her gold cross up and down the chain on her neck.

I wondered what was used in gluten-free flour if you couldn't use wheat. "Do you find that gluten-free cakes taste okay?"

Guadalupe brightened up. "Oh, yes! Chocolate banana ones are good—and I once had an angel food cake that was awesome. It was like eating a sweet cloud. But don't feel bad for me. The rice squares here are really yummy. They buy them from a gluten-free bakery someplace else. You should try one."

Since I didn't want her to feel alone, I decided against having a slice of cake with the other girls and tried a crispy rice square instead. And Guadalupe was right. It was made with brown sugar and butter and was probably the best one I'd ever tasted. I did, however, take home some of the cookies I had helped make to share with my sisters. And I wanted a fondant panda, but it didn't look like Taylor was giving them out, and anyway, they were too cute to eat. Even if she gave me one, I'd probably keep it in the freezer forever and look at it from time to time.

When the party was over, Krista and I stepped out of the bakery only to find that it was still raining. So we huddled under the awning for a minute before Hunni pulled up to the curb. "How was it?" Hunni asked when Krista and I climbed into the back seat of her car.

"Fun!" Krista crowed. And she launched into a play-by-play of the party.

Hunni interrupted her in the middle of her description of the baby pandas. "Did you have fun, too, dear?" she asked me.

"What? Mm-hmm. Yeah!" I said. And it was true enough. I *did* have fun. But I was already thinking about having to make my cinnamon rolls later. *Plus,* I realized, my heart pounding, *I still don't know how I was going to make my blondies "with a twist."*

Chapter 17

Kitty held her phone at arm's length and smiled at her own face on its screen. Then, placing a hand under her neck, showing the manicure Lena had given her earlier, she said, "Welcome to the Kitty and Cammie Show. I'm Amber Daniels, more commonly known as Kitty—"

Cammie held her phone out in much the same way and said to her screen, "Hello, and welcome to the *Cammie* and *Kitty* Show. *I'm* Ashton Daniels, although people call me Cammie—"

Kitty placed the hand with the camera on her hip. "It's the Kitty and Cammie Show!"

Cammie faced her camera at the both of them. "No, it's the Cammie and Kitty Show."

"No, it's not!" Kitty stamped a foot and turned toward me. "Come on, tell the truth, Ansley. Which sounds better? The Kitty and Cammie Show or The Cammie and Kitty Show?"

"Cammie first, obviously," said Cammie. "Besides, it's alphabetical!"

"Well, Amber comes before Ashton," Kitty pointed out.

"Girls! Girls!" I shouted. "This isn't the Cammie and Kitty or Kitty and Cammie Show!"

"She said my name first," Cammie muttered under her breath.

"It's just the video that's supposed to prove that I made the cinnamon rolls. Now, one or both of you start recording, please, or I'm going to call Dad."

"But we want to make a show," Kitty said. "And host it like *Awake with the Lake*. And we'll interview girls like us who are doing neat stuff, like you and Lena."

"And it's a very cool idea," I said, hearing my own voice getting higher and more strained, "but can you work on it later? I really need this video to enter the Bake Off." I was feeling nervous and tired, and it didn't help that my sisters weren't cooperating.

"Fine," the girls said in unison, and they both held up their camera phones at the same time.

"You know you both don't have to film it, right? One of you can film when I make the cinnamon rolls, and the other one can film when I make the blondies."

"Okay, then I'll film the cinnamon rolls," Cammie said.

"No, *I* will," Kitty exploded. "I started recording first!"

"By half a second?" Cammie challenged.

"Okay! Okay!" I gave up. "Forget it. You can *both* film me, then! I just need to get started!"

And the twins, with sidelong glances at one another, both held up their cameras at the same time again.

I took a deep breath and then, clenching my teeth in a "smile," turned first to one twin, then the other. "Hi, I'm Ansley Daniels. And I will be preparing cinnamon rolls for the first challenge of the Founder's Day Bake Off." My voice shook a tiny bit. "First, here are all my ingredients, laid out on the table. You'll see there's milk, sugar, butter, flour . . ."

Kitty and Cammie recorded me going through each step. When I finally had the rolls in the oven and set my timer, I threw myself on the couch and sighed. "Now we wait," I said. I closed my eyes for a moment and then opened them again. Both Cammie and Kitty were still recording me.

"Um, guys? You can take a break now. *I'm* going to!"

Cammie and Kitty looked at one another, each refusing to stop and waiting for the other to stop first.

I shook my head and closed my eyes again.

The next thing I knew, I could hear the kitchen timer going off.

"Wake up, Ansley! The cinnamon rolls are ready!"

I opened my eyes to see the concerned face of Kitty looming over me. I had fallen asleep on the couch! I jumped up and, with Cammie still recording me, grabbed my unicorn oven mitts and ran over to the stove.

"They look perfect," I said in relief. I almost felt like crying. I brought the pan of sweet-smelling rolls over to the kitchen counter as Kitty picked up her phone. Then, after taking a deep breath, I addressed the cameras again. "And now it's time for me to drizzle on the glaze . . ."

A few minutes later I was just saying, "And now we're done!" when my dad came into the kitchen.

"It smells great in here," he said.

"Thanks, Dad." My voice was wobbly.

"Is there something wrong?" he asked. "Cammie, you can stop now. You girls should be going to bed."

Kitty yawned. "But we're . . . supposed to record . . . the blondies."

"I can do that," Dad said. "But it's bedtime for you ladies. We're getting up early, don't forget."

The twins solemnly waved at me as they trooped up the stairs. I secretly wanted to join them.

"You look exhausted, sweetie," Dad said, putting an arm around me and pulling me into a side hug, "and these look perfect. They will be a great entry for the first challenge. You don't have to enter the second one, you know. You might even get a ribbon for these and get to enter the third challenge."

"But what if I don't? What if I don't get a ribbon, Dad?"

"Did you do your best?"

I nodded, still looking down at the glistening glaze. "Yes."

"Then I'm proud of you." Dad patted my back. "And I hope *you're* proud of you. No matter what happens."

"I still think I should make the blondies." Now my voice sounded whiny. Even to me. I really *was* tired.

Dad looked me in the eye. "Do you think you can do your best with them?"

I hesitated, then shook my head. "And I still haven't figured out the 'with a twist' part."

"Then I think it's time for you to go to bed. We'll bring the rolls to the fair early in the morning, and then you girls can enjoy the fair for a while after. How does that sound? Remember, the fair is supposed to be for having fun, not for stressing out."

I nodded again, not able to say much more. But I couldn't help wondering what Taylor was bringing to the fair. *I bet she's entering both challenges,* I thought glumly. *She's bound to get a ribbon for one of them too.*

"Come on, Ans. Let's put that away now and get some sleep."

I was feeling so exhausted that after I had brushed my teeth, changed into my pajamas, and crawled into bed, I was sure I'd fall right to sleep. Instead, I found myself staring into the dark, listening to the rain outside, and wishing I had more energy and that I had been able to think up of a way to put a "twist" on my blondie recipe. The feeling of disappointment sat like a rock in my stomach. I reached out for one of my stuffed unicorns, pulled it close to my chest, and sighed.

By morning, though, I was feeling much better. It had stopped raining and the sky outside my window was promisingly cloudless. The sleep had done me good, and I knew my cinnamon rolls had come out perfectly. Before I went downstairs, I put on my favorite unicorn T-shirt and decided that I was going to have a wonderful day.

The rest of my family seemed to be in even better moods than I was. Even though it was early, we were all kind of hyped up to be going to the fair, and there was a lot of excited energy at the table as we all laughed and chatted together over breakfast. The dogs circled around us, joining in the fun, barking, wagging their tails, and begging for scraps even though they'd been given a generous breakfast of their own. Dogs were always hungry!

Then we all piled into the minivan and headed for the fair. Inside the car, we asked Lena to sing "Happy Reunion" to us, and she sort of gave us all a lesson in harmony. We all ended up sounding awesome together. As we filled the car with music, it put me in such a good mood that I could barely remember how I'd been feeling the night before.

That is, until it was time for me to hand in my entry for the Bake Off. The parking section near the Bake Off area was muddy from the rain the night before. Before stepping out of the car, I couldn't help wishing I had worn boots instead of sneakers. And seeing other cars pulling up and all the other people stepping out of their vehicles holding *their* Bake Off entries, made my heart begin to pound.

"It's early yet, and people are still going to be setting up in some places," Dad said. "After Ansley turns in her cinnamon rolls, let's give the dogs some exercise before going into the fair."

"You should probably carry your rolls in yourself," Aunt Sam told me, handing me my tray from the trunk of the car.

As I took the rolls from her, another car pulled up next to us, and Taylor and her grandmother stepped out.

Taylor was struggling with her platter, covered in cellophane. I wasn't sure what she had made, but the dark circles under her eyes and her messy hair made it look like she had stayed up half the night making it. She had flour stains on her clothes, though, that made me think maybe she had just gotten up early to make her entry instead.

That would mean they're really fresh, I thought.

Her grandmother, Lynda Lang, greeted all of us. She took a quick look at my tray, which was covered in aluminum foil. Then she introduced herself to my dad and Aunt Sam.

I nodded at Taylor. "Hi, Tay—"

"*Oh*, no, you don't!" Taylor shouted. "Not again!" Her eyes were wide and wild as she stared down at Zette and Austin who had just leapt out of the car. They were jumping and loping around, enjoying the sensation of the mud on the bottoms of their paws. "Get away!" Taylor cried. Then, keeping one hand on the back door of the car to support herself and the other hand clutching her dish of freshly baked goods, she kicked her foot out a few times. "Shoo! *Shoo!*"

"Hey!" I growled. "Don't do that! You're going to hurt one of them!"

But she kept jutting her foot out over and over while the dogs jumped around her, barking and panting.

"Taylor! Stop it!" I bent down to try to hold them back and to make sure she didn't kick either of them in the face. Then, trying to back away from her foot, Austin jumped backwards into me, knocking into the arm holding the cinnamon rolls.

"No!" I yelled. But it was too late, my tray of cinnamon rolls fell facedown in the mud.

I might still be able to save a couple, I thought desperately, since they were covered in aluminum foil, but then both dogs fell upon the rolls and gobbled them up as if we had starved them for a week. I could hear my aunt scream as my dad tried to pull the dogs off.

Taylor ducked back inside her car and locked the door while her grandmother watched the drama unfold. "Such a shame," she said, in a voice that made me think she didn't think it was a shame at all. "Such beautiful looking cinnamon rolls too."

Then she walked around her car, got Taylor to come out the other side, and said loudly, "We'd better check in before something like that happens to us!" She waved goodbye to us. "So sorry!"

I watched in shock and sadness as they headed toward the sign-in tent with Taylor's grandmother wrapping an arm protectively around Taylor's shoulders. And just as I was going to look away from them, Taylor turned around, caught my eye, and mouthed, "Now you know how it feels."

I gasped, and once I saw the two of them reach the tent, I threw myself in the back seat of our car and slammed the door. I just wanted to cry.

"Ansley?" Dad knocked on the window of the car. "Ansley, honey, open up."

I shook my head and covered my face with my hands.

"Ansley!" Lena called from the other side.

"Lena," Dad said, "How about you just take Austin out of here?"

I could hear Lena grunt as she tried to convince Austin that his cinnamon-y treat was finished. "Come on, boy. You ate it all. Now you're going to have to work it off."

"Come on, Zette," Aunt Sam said. "Come on, girl."

I heard a car pull up on our other side and its doors pop open. "We saw what happened," Hunni's voice floated into my left ear. "It was terrible! Poor Ansley!"

"She's very upset," I heard Dad say. "She worked so hard on those cinnamon rolls."

"Oh!" Krista exclaimed. "And those are so good."

"Yeah," Kitty agreed sadly from somewhere behind the car. "Too bad the judges won't ever know just *how* good."

They'll never know, I thought, with a sinking heart. *They'll never kn*—I popped my head up. *Wait a minute.*

I scrambled back out of the car.

"Dad! Dad!" I was so excited that my hands were moving in the air like I was trying to pull the words out of my mouth. "Take me home!"

"I understand, sweetie, but your sisters . . ."

"I can take her back," Aunt Sam said. "Oh, I wish we had thought to bring both cars!"

"I can do it," Hunni said. "I can drive you both back, if you want. Then if Ansley wants to return to the fair, you can drive back in your own car," she told Aunt Sam.

"Oh, I'll *want* to come back," I broke in. "In fact, I'll *need* to—with my entry for the second challenge!"

143

My friends and family stared at me, looking stunned to see the smile on my face instead of tears in my eyes.

"I know just what I'm going to bake too," I said, rubbing my hands together eagerly. "Blondies . . . with a twist."

Chapter 18

"Okay," I said as I looked over my ingredients and my large mixing bowl on the kitchen counter. "I know it's a great idea, but how do I make it? How do I create a combination cinnamon roll-blondie? A 'cinnamondie!'" I giggled nervously. "Well, let me just start mixing the blondie ingredients." I looked up at my aunt. "You're taping this, right?"

She gave me a thumbs-up as she watched me on the screen of her smart phone.

"Good. Okay. I know what I'll do. Since I can't roll up blondie dough in a swirl like a cinnamon roll, I *can* swirl cinnamon *filling* into the blondie *batter!* Yes!" I jumped up and down in place. "And then when the blondies are done, I'll drizzle on the glaze as usual. Oh, this is going to taste awesome."

"Remember," my aunt said as she continued to film me, "you can enter up to a dozen blondies in the challenge, but no more."

"I *am* making a dozen," I said.

"Yes, but if you want to taste them, or let your family taste them, maybe you should make more?"

"Good point," I said, getting a second mixing bowl out of one of the cabinets. "I think I'll double the recipe. I have the feeling we're all going to enjoy these. Not to mention, maybe I'll need a backup batch, just in case something happens to the first one!"

"Now you're cooking with gas!" Aunt Sam said approvingly.

"Literally!" we said together.

I had a lot of fun racing the clock as I created my cinna-mondies. And when both batches were done, Aunt Sam and I tasted a sample from each in case we found one batch better than the other.

My aunt closed her eyes after taking a bite from the first batch. "Mmmm! That's heaven!"

I took a bite from the second. "So's this one!"

It wasn't easy to choose which batch to enter—they were both so good. In the end, we decided it didn't really matter which. So once we chose one, I sliced it up into bars and packed them up securely—first in wax paper, then in aluminum foil, and finally in a sealed container. I wasn't going to go through a doggie disaster again!

When Aunt Sam and I returned to the Bake Off area, there was a long line of people waiting to enter their dishes into the second challenge. As we inched our way toward the sign-in tent, I gripped my blondies as if my life depended on them getting to the tent. I kept my eyes closed most of the time and prayed hard. *Please God, don't let anything happen to these blondies. Let me enter them into the contest. Whether I win or lose is not up to me, but I at least want to have a chance!* Then, feeling Aunt Sam nudge me, I opened my eyes.

Lynda and Taylor Lang were leaving the tent. Taylor had her head held up high as she carried a silver tray with two ribbons dangling from it. One said "Freshness" and the other said "Texture."

"She's got two ribbons," I said grimly. "That means she'll be in the cake contest tomorrow."

"Looks like it," Aunt Sam said as we watched a man holding a camera with the words *Awake with the Lake* written on its side and a woman holding a microphone jogging after the Langs. The woman was calling out to them to stop for a moment. "And whether you get in the cake contest or not," Aunt Sam said, "can you at least say you did your best with these blondies?"

"You mean my cinnamondies?" I nudged her back in a joking way.

"Yes. Did you do your best with them?"

"Yes, ma'am." Just remembering how good they tasted made me want to go back home and devour the other batch that was still there.

"Then that's what counts. If there's a ribbon for effort you should certainly get that." Aunt Sam gave my shoulders a supportive squeeze.

When we got to the front of the line and I gave my name at the table, the lady taking down my information looked up at me in surprise. "Ansley Daniels? Oh! I'm happy to see you! We heard about your accident this morning from your father. I'm so glad to see you've come back to give it another try. Good for you!"

"Thanks," I said, standing up a little straighter. Hearing her say that was almost like getting a ribbon for not giving up.

Once we took care of all the paperwork, left the blondies (in an attractive arrangement) for judging, and left the tent, I dusted my hands together. "Well, that's that."

"If you get a ribbon, we won't know for a couple of hours, so why not have some fun at the fair?" Aunt Sam said, lifting her cell phone up. "Your dad said that he and your sisters are all at the picnic tables nearest to the track."

When we found them, they were eating hot dogs and ice cream. My sisters had their faces painted and looked a little tired.

"Looks like you've all been having fun without me," I said, trying not to sound too disappointed.

"We went on some rides," Kitty said.

"And got to ride horses," Cammie added.

"I helped judge the first karaoke contest of the day," Lena said.

"And we got to make these neat beaded bracelets," Cammie said, sticking out her arm to show me the blue beads circling her wrist. "We made one for you too."

Kitty licked her chocolate ice cream cone and pointed to Lena. "She has it."

Lena took it out of her pocket and handed it to me.

"Thanks," I said, rolling the pink and purple bracelet onto my wrist. Part of me really wished I had gotten the chance to make my own bracelet. The other part of me was glad that my sisters hadn't forgotten about me, at least. "I see you all got your faces painted too."

"We can show you where the face painter is," Lena said, looking past Aunt Sam to find the booth.

"Your sisters are kind of tired," Dad said. "We can come back tonight for some more events. They're having music, a bonfire, that sort of thing. But I think they need a nap after getting up so early. Do you want to stay for a little while with your Aunt Sam and check out the fair?"

"I guess," I said, tracing zig-zag lines on the grass with the toe of my sneaker. The fair just wouldn't be as much fun without my sisters.

Suddenly a voice cried out, "Ansley!" and I saw Guadalupe running toward me.

"I just got here," she said a little breathlessly when she reached me. Then she looked at Lena, Cammie, and Kitty. "Oh, but you've been here a while, haven't you?"

"No," I said. "*They* have, but I haven't!"

"Oh, good! Then do you wanna hang out with me? I just passed the face-painting booth over there. Look, you can see Nikki and her sisters going there now."

"Can I, Dad?" I asked.

"I'll keep an eye on her," Aunt Sam said. "We want to hang around for the judging, anyway."

So Dad let me stay, and I got to have fun with Guadalupe. We had tiaras painted on our foreheads. We participated in a hula-hooping contest, we tried the Ferris wheel, admired all the beautiful flowers in the flower show, we got to paint rocks with inspirational messages (to take home with us), and we even got to mix up and drink smoothies. Guadalupe was lots of fun to hang around with. She was pretty much game for anything. The only sad part about being with her at a fair was that there was a lot of food she couldn't eat. So much of the food was covered in flour or dough or came in buns. I had never realized how much wheat was in food until I spent a day with someone who couldn't eat it without getting sick.

But at least she could have the smoothie. After drinking hers, Guadalupe sat down on the grass and pointed across the field. "Hey, do you want to try joining in one of those relay races?"

I plopped down beside her. "Are you kidding? Aren't you too full from that smoothie?"

Guadalupe sat back a little and stuck out her tongue. "Actually, yeah."

"I'm not going to get up from here for at least an hour," I claimed with a groan.

"Actually, we're going to have to leave soon," Aunt Sam said with a little groan herself. She had just settled onto a picnic table bench behind us. "You two have one more rehearsal with the Gracelets for tomorrow's performance, remember? And we have to pick up that leotard so that you can match the other girls."

"Oh, right!"

"But first, let's just relax for a few minutes." Aunt Sam sighed.

I closed my eyes and just enjoyed the feeling of the sun on my face for a moment. Then something made me open my eyes in time to see a girl about my age walking past us. She was holding some kind of sealed food container and exclaiming over the blue ribbon on it that had the word "Presentation" written across it.

"Aunt Sam! Look!" I jumped to my feet. "The judging must be over!"

Aunt Samantha looked at her watch. "Must be."

"Come on!" I waved for her and Guadalupe to follow me. "Let's go!"

Even though I ran all the way to the tent, when I got to it, I couldn't go in without backup. So I waited for Aunt Sam and Guadalupe to catch up with me before going inside. "There it is . . . that's the place I left my blondies," I said, covering one side of my face as I inched closer to the table. "I can't look!"

Guadalupe gasped. "Look! Look, Ansley!"

"Go ahead, honey, it's all right," Aunt Sam said, gently prying my hand away from my face.

There on the dish (with only six blondies out of twelve on it) next to a place card with my name on it were two ribbons. One read "Taste" and the other read "Freshness."

A woman wearing a ribbon on her chest that said "Judge" came toward me with an apologetic smile. "Sorry we ate half of them, but after one bite I couldn't stop myself from eating a whole blondie. My fellow judges all seemed to have the same problem. They were very good, young lady."

"Thanks!" I gushed.

"I was wondering," she asked with her hands behind her back like a small child. "Could I take one or two home with me? I'd love for my husband to try one, and I'd like to save another for tomorrow. I bet it would taste wonderful warmed up a bit and with a cup of coffee."

"Sure! I mean, please do." I gestured toward the plate and admitted with a chuckle, "I have more at home, anyway."

"Oh, thank you!" The judge took a napkin and put one, two, *three* blondies in it. Then, with a wink at me, she walked away. And it looked to me like she was trying to secretly take a bite out of one before she'd even left the tent.

Aunt Sam took my hands in hers just as the cameraman and interviewer from *Awake with the Lake* came over to us. "You did it, Ansley! You've qualified for the cake contest! Congratulations!"

Guadalupe looked longingly at my prize-winning blondies. "I wish I could try them."

"Do we have permission to record your daughter?" the interviewer asked, even though it was obvious by the light shining in my face that they were already doing that.

"She's my beloved niece," Aunt Sam corrected her, "but yes."

"You've qualified for the third baking challenge in the junior division," the lady said. "How do you feel about that?"

"Excited, I guess," I said. Trying not to squint at the brightness of the spotlight, I decided to focus on the lipstick stain on the lady's teeth.

"To win that challenge, you'll have to whip up a cake that everybody loves." She went on, "Something worthy to be called 'Fair Favorite.' Do you think you're up to the challenge?"

I swallowed hard. "I think so . . . I hope so . . . I'm gonna try."

The television woman was tall, and in her high heels, especially so. She bent down to get the microphone even closer to my face and asked brightly, "Do you have any idea what you're going to make?"

"I didn't until just now, actually," I said, flashing a sidelong glance at Guadalupe. "But yes, I do. And it's going to be a surprise."

"Hmm. Sounds special," the TV lady said. "Can you give us even a tiny hint?"

"Nope! You'll have to wait until tomorrow." I laughed. "But to make it happen . . ." I looked up at Aunt Sam. "I think we're going to need to go to the store."

Chapter 19

When Aunt Sam and I came through the door, we were greeted by cheers, barking dogs, and a sign on the wall that said "Congratulations, Ansley!" with drawings of cupcakes and cookies around the letters.

"What's all this?" I asked. "The cake challenge isn't even until tomorrow, and I might not even win that!"

"It's for your ribbons, of course," Dad said, giving me a hug.

My sisters all followed me to the kitchen counter and watched me take out my new tube pan, mixing bowl, and utensils.

"You have all these already," Lena said, turning the mixing bowl over and around. "Why did you get more?"

"Because my recipe calls for . . ." I lifted out a small sack of cornstarch from the shopping bag and laid it on the counter, "gluten-free ingredients. I can't use the stuff that's touched wheat."

"Gluten free?" Cammie made a face. "Will it taste any good?"

"Hopefully like sweet clouds," I said, taking out two cartons of eggs from the bag. "It's going to be an angel food cake."

"Are you sure you want to do angel food? It can be kind of plain," Aunt Sam warned.

"But with the right amount of butter and vanilla, it can be quite tasty," Dad pointed out.

"Plus," I said, taking out a carton of strawberries, "I'm going to top it with these and make whipped cream to serve with it."

"That should be a crowd-pleaser," Dad said approvingly.

"And with *more* of the crowd able to eat it," Lena said, crossing her arms, "more people will be able to like it. You might have a real chance of winning 'Favorite of the Fair.'"

"That *is* the idea," I said. "But I also wanted to make something Guadalupe could eat and enjoy."

"Are you going to use any frosting?" Kitty asked.

"I'm not sure. The whipped cream might be enough. Or maybe I'll whip up a light and fluffy version of buttercream frosting for the top only. I haven't decided yet. I'll just bring the ingredients and make my decision when I'm there, I guess." I sighed. "You know what I really wish? That I could make a unicorn cake. You should have seen the adorable pandas Taylor made with fondant. I can't do anything like that."

"Maybe you can stick an upside-down ice cream cone on top of it," Cammie suggested. "You know, like a horn."

"Hey! Yeah!" I liked that idea.

"No, honey," Dad shook his head. "Ice cream cones are made with wheat flour. They are not gluten-free."

"Oh." I slumped in my seat.

Undaunted, Cammie thought of something else. "Maybe you can use a unicorn cookie cutter and cut out a unicorn-shaped piece of cake?"

I liked that idea, too, until I remembered that angel food cakes needed to be made in tube pans, and I wouldn't have a layer to spare.

"You can use the cookie cutter on fondant, though, couldn't you?" Lena asked, taking the unicorn-shaped cookie cutter from the drawer.

"That might work!" I said. I tried to imagine where I would

put the fondant, though. It seemed kind of heavy for the top of the cake. *Maybe I can arrange the shapes around the cake? Like a carousel?* "I'll take this cookie cutter with me," I decided, and Lena slipped it into a plastic baggie for me. "I'll also have to take ingredients to make fondant. Thanks, Lena and Cammie."

"What about," Kitty said, opening a cabinet and taking a small shaker out of it, "using rainbow sprinkles in the batter? That will make your cake more . . . unicorn-ish." She handed me the small bottle of sprinkles.

"I think you're right," I said, shaking up the sprinkles inside the bottle a little. "I'll bring these too. Thanks!"

"Uh-oh!" Lena looked at the clock on the microwave. "Gotta run! Mallory's going to video chat with me in Dad's office, so we can rehearse. She's even going to let me play the guitar along with her! Talk to you later!" Lena hurried off.

"Maybe we can film her rehearsal!" Cammie said to Kitty, and the two of them followed behind her.

Dad started heating up some pasta for me. "You've had a long day," he said as I climbed onto one of the saddle stools at our kitchen counter. "And you're going to have another long one tomorrow. You best get to bed early tonight."

"I know," I said. "I will."

As Aunt Sam began putting away the groceries, I pulled the small sack of gluten-free all-purpose flour across the counter and took it in both my hands. A gluten-free cake had been a spur-of-the-moment decision. I hoped it would be the right one.

I'm sure Taylor won't be making one, anyway, I thought to myself, *but I wonder what she* will *make!*

The next morning, my whole family was up early again. Before we all left for the fair, Dad had us form a circle and hold hands with one another as he prayed, "Father, my family comes before you united in love for one another as you call us to be. We thank you for the abundance of blessings you have poured out upon us as a family and we praise you for your goodness. Today as we accompany Ansley and Lena to the fair, we ask you to help them use their gifts to the best of their abilities and that you accept them as offerings of thanksgiving from them. And let them—and all my girls—have lots of fun today!"

And the Daniels sisters all said loudly, "Amen!"

"And please bless Dad," I added quickly. "He works so hard and has been so good to us. Please continue to give him strength and guidance and love, in Jesus' name. Amen!"

And my sisters said even more loudly this time, "Amen!"

When we got to the tents set up for the cake challenge, we found that there were cameras and lights set up all around the area. There were also long tables for all the competitors to work at and brand-new ovens supplied by a sponsor of *Awake with the Lake.*

The cameraman and interviewer from yesterday were also there. The woman was wearing a bright green jacket and skirt that made her really stand out, so she was easy to spot walking around.

Parents and family were allowed to sit on bleachers off to the side and watch. All the participants in the contest had to submit their recipes and get approval before we were given aprons and chef hats just like at Lynda's Lovin' Oven, except this time they were orange, and all said "Awake with the Lake" on them. Then we were led to our stations, where I found myself in the same row as Taylor, who had been assigned to the place on my right. I immediately said "Hi" to her. She jumped and nodded her "hello" back, but didn't say a word.

I bet she's surprised to see me here, I thought. *She probably thought when my cinnamon rolls were ruined that I was out of the running.*

The judges came out and introduced themselves. There were a total of five. Each was responsible for a different blue ribbon: Taste, Texture, Originality, Presentation, and Freshness. Our cakes, they told us, would be judged as before, except the Favorite of the Fair would be judged by ordinary fairgoers who, for a window of time, would get to visit the tent and sample tiny bites of our cakes. No one from the bleachers would be allowed to vote!

Cammie and Kitty looked disgruntled to hear that. I think they at least wanted to taste the cake I made when it was done.

After the rules were explained, the lady judge who had walked away with three of my blondies started the challenge by shouting, "On your mark, get set . . . Bake Off!"

All the kids surrounding me pounced on their ingredients and hurriedly got to work. But I knew I had plenty of time to get things done, and I didn't want to rush myself and make a mistake. So I tried to be as careful and steady as I could. Separating fourteen yolks from egg whites takes some concentration, after all.

As we worked, the interviewer from the TV station started talking to people in the bleachers. Then, after some time had passed, she began going around to each competitor and asking them questions. I found this a little annoying, since I thought we all needed to focus on our work and felt like she was being kind of distracting. She asked the bakers things like what they were working on and what their hopes and dreams were—and I couldn't help overhearing some of them.

In one conversation, I found out that the girl I had seen yesterday walking away with a ribbon that said "Presentation" on it, was named June. And when she described the chocolate-ginger sponge cake she was making, it sounded so delicious that I was sure she would win. Then the interviewer (whose name was Sierra Li) spoke to a boy named Caden who was making a chocolate cake with coffee-flavored frosting and bacon bits sprinkled on it. When Sierra heard about *that*, she said she definitely wanted to try it when it was done. A pair of sisters (I didn't know that competitors could be a team) were making a hummingbird cake with bananas, pineapple, and pecans. Sierra practically drooled over each ingredient in that one. After a while, it sounded to me like each cake was as at least as good or better than the last one. Sierra hadn't even interviewed half of the other contestants before I was sure I wasn't going to win the competition.

But what I can do, I told myself, *is my best—and . . . have fun, of course!* And it *was* fun mixing the batter and watching it get beautifully light and fluffy. *Sweet clouds*, I thought with a smile. My cake was in the oven and I was about to make fondant by the time Sierra came to my row. I almost jumped when I heard her voice to my right ask, "Is that fondant you're using?"

I turned to tell her that I hadn't even started making it yet when I saw that she was actually speaking to Taylor, who was bent over little sculptures she was working on.

Taylor lifted her head. "Yes, it's fondant." She lifted the figure she had just completed and held it up to the camera. "They're unicorns!"

Chapter 20

I felt my stomach drop.

"They're absolutely adorable!" Sierra cooed.

"Thank you!" Taylor giggled and went back to concentrating on what she was doing. I could see that she had finished two unicorns and was working on a third. They were as adorable as Sierra said, with wavy manes in rainbow colors and golden swirly horns.

"So what kind of cake will these little cuties be decorating?"

Please don't say an angel food cake! I prayed in my mind. *Pleeeeease don't say an angel food cake!*

"Lemon poppy seed," Taylor said, "with cream cheese frosting. It's my mom's—*was* my mom's—favorite."

"Oh . . . yes," Sierra's big smile fell away as she pressed her lips together to show sympathy. "I was sorry to hear that you lost your mother this summer. How are you doing?"

I frowned. *Sierra is obviously confusing Taylor with me.*

But Taylor shrugged. "Okay, I guess."

"Do you find that baking helps when you feel sad?"

"Sure," she said, smiling down at the unicorn that seemed to magically appear between her fluttering hands. "And art too."

After Sierra observed Taylor at work for a few minutes, she said, "You're really good at that, Taylor. Perhaps you should go into the cake decorating business professionally when you grow up."

Taylor pointed to her grandmother in the stands. "Well, my grandmother does have a bakery. She says she'll give it to me once I graduate. She was going to leave it to my mom, but . . . you know."

I couldn't believe what I was hearing. Taylor had lost her mom like I had. And very recently too.

Sierra caught me watching them. "And you're Ansley, right?"

The camera and spotlight turned toward me. "Yes, ma'am."

"And are you going to make something with fondant too?"

I shook my head and slid the bag of marshmallows I was going to use to make the fondant away from view. *Not anymore, I'm not.*

I saw Taylor hunch her shoulders as she stole a glance at me and began making another unicorn.

"And what kind of cake are you making?" Sierra asked me.

"Angel food," I said. "Gluten-free, actually, so my friend Guadalupe can have some—and maybe other people at this fair who can't eat the other cakes."

"How thoughtful of you. And smart. It's an option that the others haven't thought of. More people will be able to sample your cake that way."

"I hope so," I said. "Of course, people will have to find out that the cake is even here before they can try it!"

Sierra chuckled. "That's true. Still, I think it's good of you to think of others and their special needs when you're in the middle of trying to win a contest. Especially when you don't have those same needs. You don't have a gluten allergy, do you?"

I inhaled deeply, taking in the smells of all the baking cakes around me—and the faint smell of burnt crust. "No, I don't," I admitted.

"Your dad is impressed too. I spoke with him earlier—as well as all your sisters. They are all proud of you for both making it into this competition and for thinking of your friend. You have a very supportive family."

"I know," I said.

"It's good that you all have each other to lean on since you're all going through something so very much like what Taylor's going through."

From the corner of my eye I saw Taylor freeze in place.

"Was angel food *your* mother's favorite cake?" Sierra went on.

"No," I said, noticing the burnt smell getting a little stronger. "But she was the one who taught me how to bake."

"Well, I'm sure she'd be as proud of you as the rest of your family is to see how far your baking talents have taken—" Suddenly Sierra sniffed the air. "Something's burning."

"Oh, no!" Taylor cried out. She ran to her oven, threw open the door, and reached in for her cake pan without wearing an oven mitt. Burning herself slightly, she hissed in pain from the sting, ran back to the table to retrieve her mitt, and then went back to the stove. She reminded me of a tennis ball, first flying in one direction and then in the opposite direction and back again. When she finally got her cake out of the oven, it was too late. The top and edges were brown and crispy. She burst into tears.

The cameraman, who had been recording the whole drama, moved in closer.

"Taylor!" I ran over to her and put an arm around her

161

shoulders. "Please, get that thing away from her," I told the cameraman. "Can't you see she's upset?"

Sierra waved at the cameraman to back up a bit, and they gave Taylor some space as she sank into a nearby chair. "I can't believe I let that happen! It's completely ruined!"

I squatted down so that I could look up into her crumpled face. "I'm sorry that happened, Taylor. I'm really sorry." I felt so bad for her. I wished I could make it better.

"*You're* sorry?" Taylor blinked down at me. "*I'm* the one who's sorry! I'm the one who—who—" And suddenly I knew we weren't talking about cakes anymore. "Is it true?" she asked with a sniff. "Did you really lose your mom too?"

I felt my eyes grow wet. "Yes."

"I didn't know," Taylor said.

"I didn't know about your mom, either."

"Don't you miss her?" Taylor's voice broke a little.

"All the time. Every minute," I admitted.

"Then . . . how can you smile all the time?"

"I don't know. Maybe . . . maybe because I have the gift of joy." Taylor looked confused.

"Dad says it's from the Holy Spirit," I explained. "But I also smile because my family and I talk about her a lot and remember the good times we had with her. There are a *lot* of good times to remember. Can you do that with memories of your mom?"

Taylor sniffed again, but the tiniest of smiles twitched at the ends of her mouth. "Yes. But you're so lucky. You have a lot of people you can talk to and who understand. I only have Grandma."

"You also have Krista," I reminded her. "She's your best friend. I'm sure she listens to you."

"She does, but she doesn't always understand. I don't think she likes it when I'm sad."

"Well . . . now you have me too. You can always talk to me. You know I'll understand. And it's okay to be sad, you know. It's okay to cry."

Taylor nodded. "That's what my counselor always says."

"And, of course, I know I'll see my mom again someday. And you'll see yours. That's the best part!"

"Do you really believe that?" Taylor's voice grew high and hopeful.

"Oh, yes. I do. I really do." The timer on my oven went off. "Oh!" I jumped up.

"You'd better get that before your cake is ruined too," Taylor said, sounding sad again. She got up out of her chair and began to undo her apron.

"Taylor," I said, as I headed over to my oven. "Do you . . . do you want to help me finish this cake? Maybe we can enter it together as a team. You can make the frosting, and even spread it on the cake, if you want. And decorate it with your unicorns! Do you want to?"

Taylor's mouth formed an "o" at the thought. "Can we even do that? I mean, won't we be disqualified or something?"

"Well, those two sisters over there are working together," I said as I carefully placed my cake upside down on its cooling rack.

Taylor looked tempted for a moment, then she shook her head. "I wouldn't want to get you in trouble or kicked out of the contest or anything."

I waved my hand. "I don't care about that," I said, and I meant it. Suddenly, being kind to Taylor when she most needed it seemed *way* more important than winning a ribbon or a trophy. And making a cake with her (and her fondant unicorns!) seemed a lot more fun than getting on a TV show too. "Come on! I bet you can make a really fluffy icing. It would make the perfect clouds for your unicorns to prance around. And it would still be gluten-free . . ."

Taylor's eyes danced as she tied her apron more firmly around her waist. "Okay! Let's do it!"

The judges allowed us to become a team, but warned us we might run into a problem if we won. "Who would keep the trophy?" they asked.

Taylor and I didn't have the answer to that. But the question made me kind of hope we didn't win after all.

When Taylor finished decorating the cake, it looked super cute. She made five unicorns altogether, but instead of putting them on top of the cake and weighing down the fluff, she put them around the cake, sort of like the carousel idea I had the night before. "This unicorn is me," she said, "this one is you. This one is Guadalupe, this one is Krista, and this last one is Nikki."

"Nikki!" I said. I began to untie my apron with shaking hands. "I've got to perform with her and Guadalupe with the Gracelets soon! Let's hand this cake in because I've got to run. And I know you don't like gymnastics much, but I think you should come and watch because of what will happen afterwards. There's going to be a cool, secret surprise!"

"Actually, I think gymnastics is okay." Taylor looked a little embarrassed.

I smiled. "Go get Krista, and head over to the bandstand. She'll like the surprise too."

"Okay!"

The Gracelets performance was just part of a longer performance piece where different groups of gymnasts from Grace-n-Power each had time to show off their skills and publicize the work of the gym. Nikki, Guadalupe, and the other Gracelets did an awesome job with their ribbon routine, and each time I made a tumbling pass I could hear the unmistakable hoots and whistles from my personal cheering section of family and friends.

Nikki, Guadalupe, and I found Taylor and Krista in the audience afterwards. "Wait until you see this!" I told them as Lena's choir assembled on the stage. They performed a beautiful arrangement of Mallory Winston's song, "Forever Grateful," and once they got to the last stanza, Mallory *herself* came out onstage and joined in! The crowd roared their welcome. The choir looked shocked, but they managed to continue without missing a beat, and by the end, Mallory, the choir, and the audience were all singing together.

Then, before Mallory and Lena sang their duet, Mallory introduced the song saying, "This next song is my newest single, and it's dedicated to the memory of a very special lady, Mrs. Eva Daniels. She was the mother of Lena, who is my singing partner tonight, and who starred with me in *Above the Waters* a few years back. Mrs. Daniels was a great woman of faith whose love for her family and example to her daughters impressed me very much when I met her. She is with the Lord now, but we all look forward to the day when we can meet her again in the 'Happy Reunion . . .'"

They sang it twice, so that by the second time the audience could sing along to some of the chorus. I could see that a lot of people were touched by the lyrics. Taylor and I weren't the only ones who had lost people we loved, and the song comforted them and gave them hope. I particularly liked a part that went:

We'll sit together at the table
Down from the first up to the least
And all partake together
Of the Bridegroom's happy feast.

It made me picture heaven as one big party, and I imagined my mom and Taylor's mom as two friends, sitting side by side, clinking their drinking glasses together as part of the celebration.

When the performance was over, Dad ushered us away from the bandstand and toward the Bake Off tents. "Okay, girls," he said. "I think it's time for the judging."

When we got back, I was almost too nervous to look again, but Taylor grabbed my arm and brought me over to our presentation station. There, next to what was left of the cake, we found three blue ribbons! One for "Taste," one for "Presentation," and one for "Originality."

"Look at all the ribbons you got!" said Taylor, who was still holding on to my arm and jumping up and down.

"You mean *we* got," I corrected her.

Then it was finally time for the "Favorite of the Fair" announcement. Taylor squeezed her eyes shut and crossed her fingers. I closed my eyes too, but when I did, I realized I didn't really want to win anymore. I found instead that becoming friends with Taylor, performing with Grace-n-Power, and enjoying Mallory's surprise duet with Lena had all contributed to putting a joy in my heart that was even bigger than the trophy that would go to the winner.

"And the trophy goes to . . ." the announcer paused. Then, "Dagny Roberts and her triple layer red velvet cake!"

As Dagny's family and friends cheered, Taylor and I looked at one another.

"Dagny? Who's Dagny?" I asked.

"I have no idea," Taylor said.

We both burst out laughing. "Oh, well," I said. "Better luck next time! We still got a lot of blue ribbons!"

"Yeah," Taylor said. "Because our cake was awesome!"

"Especially your unicorns." I bent down for another look at them. I must not have been the only person who thought that they were too cute to eat. "Can I take the 'Ansley' unicorn home?"

"Sure!"

As I carefully transferred the fondant cutie onto another plate, I waved Guadalupe over. "Let me cut you a nice piece," I said, "since I made it gluten-free just for you."

Guadalupe gasped. "Really? Wow! That is *so* nice of you! Thanks!" When she took a bite out of the fluffy, white wedge, her face took on a blissful expression. "So good. Just like—"

"Sweet clouds, I hope!" I said.

Just then, Lena, Cammie, and Kitty gathered around us.

"Can your sisters get a piece too?" Cammie asked.

"Of course," I said, and I began slicing small pieces for them all. "You deserve one for all the help you gave me with ideas and stuff. In fact . . ."

I plucked the blue ribbon for "Originality" up and stuck it on Cammie. "Thank you for all the cake decorating ideas and for recording me and for your advice and everything."

"You're welcome." Cammie smiled proudly.

Then I grabbed the blue ribbon for "Taste" and stuck it on

Kitty. "Thank you for the sprinkles and also for recording and for all your support."

"You're welcome," Kitty said shyly.

Last, I stuck the blue ribbon for "Presentation" on Lena. "And that is for your performance today! It was amazing! Plus, you deserve it for praying with me and well . . . just for all your help!"

"Three blue ribbons for three true-blue sisters!" I thrust my arm out in the middle of our circle. "Even in times when we're apart, the Daniels sisters promise with all our hearts . . ."

My sisters all joined in. "That we'll always be . . . Together *four*-ever! Together *four*-ever! Together *four*-ever! Together *four*-ever!"

We cheered and jumped up and down.

"Come on, Daniels sisters," Dad said, wrapping his arms around the four of us as best he could. "Let's find a good place to eat together. Mallory said to just let her know where and she'll join us. What about you, Taylor? Would you and your grandmother like to come with us? Guadalupe?"

"Yeah, guys," I said, excitedly. "The more the merrier. Let's make it a big party! Like a heavenly feast!" And we all began singing "Happy Reunion" as we headed off toward the picnic section to look for the perfect table to seat us all.

Read this excerpt from Book 2
in the Daniels Sisters Series:

Ashton's Dancing Dreams

Chapter 1

My dad, sisters, and I were all in the car, just about to pull up to school, when my favorite song came on the radio—"God is Good," by our favorite singer, Mallory Winston.

"Oooh! Turn it up! Turn it up, Daddy!" My three sisters all spoke at once.

Ansley started swaying to the music. Lena (my oldest sister) and Amber (my twin) started singing along. I closed my eyes to listen to the lyrics:

> They gave me the bad news
> And I didn't know what to do.
> And I wondered what to say
> Do I laugh or do I cry?
> Do I scream or do I sigh?
> Or I just kneel down and pray?

As I kept my eyes closed, I imagined a dance to go along with the words to the song. Daydreaming like this had become one of my favorite things to do lately. It was fun for me because I was taking classes in lyrical dance (a way of acting out a story with dance moves) and I loved it!

The daydream usually went like this: I would be standing on a stage, silently waiting in the dark. Suddenly, the spotlight would come on and focus right on me, making the sequins in my pink dance outfit shimmer ever so slightly. Then the music would begin. I could just picture the exact arm gestures I would do to the opening line "When they gave me the bad news." Then I would do a half-turn on "I didn't know what do." I would flip my hands up on "Was there something I should say?" and would, of course, fall to my knees on "or should I just kneel down and pray." Next, I would leap . . .

"Cammie!" a voice called me from far off in the distance. (Cammie is my family nickname.)

My eyes were still closed as I made a joyful leap across the stage . . .

"Cammie!"

Now I was hunching my back and covering my face with my hands . . .

"Ashton Joy Daniels!"

Uh-Oh. The music had been shut off and Dad had used my full name. I popped my eyes open and met his gaze in the rear-view mirror. "Yeah, Dad?"

"Will you be joining your sisters in school today? Or were you planning on coming back home with me?"

I giggled and unbuckled my backseat belt. "I guess I'll be joining my sisters."

"Good idea," Dad said, nodding. I watched the reflection of his eyes as they crinkled in a smile.

"Come *on*, Cammie!" Amber called to me from outside. I popped out of the car and hurried to catch up with her. We were not identical twins, so we didn't look alike. People had no problem telling us apart. But they were always comparing us to one another anyway. Like, "Oh, she's the shy one and you're the more outgoing one." Or "She likes singing and you like dancing."

My favorite one though was when someone called Amber "sugar and spice" and me "fire and ice." I liked the sound of that! Anyway, I guess when you're sisters, people are always going to compare you to each other, whether you are twins or not.

"What happened? Did you forget something?" Amber wrinkled her forehead with the question.

"Yeah," I said. "I forgot to get out of the car!"

We followed Lena and Ansley as they walked through the opened front gates of our school campus, Roland Lake Christian Academy. The school was made up of three buildings. The main building was a big, old-fashioned mansion with white columns, and two other brick buildings stood one on either side of it. The middle building actually *was* the middle school, and Ansley dashed off to meet her friends there. Lena veered off to the left, toward the high school. Amber and I headed to the right, toward the elementary school building. But since students from all three schools were gathered together on the front lawn, we could all hear greetings to each one of us coming from different directions. Everyone knew us Daniels sisters because there were four of us and we were the only set of siblings that year who were attending classes in all three buildings.

"Ashton! Amber!" Our friends Esperanza Harrison and June Harlow called out to us.

We waved at them and stopped walking to allow the girls time to run over and join us. Rani (which is what we called Esperanza) and June were really best friends to each other, just like Amber and I were. But at school a lot of the time Rani was more like my best friend and June was Amber's. June had pale, reddish-blonde, wispy hair that she usually wore in a simple ponytail, very light blue eyes, and eyelashes that were almost silver. Rani was practically her opposite. She had dark hair that she wore in two thick braids, super dark eyebrows, super dark eyelashes, and eyes that were almost black. But today, by the time she reached me and came to a panting stop, I could see that her eyes were looking red . . . and puffy

"What's wrong? Are you okay?" I asked.

Rani nodded as she caught her breath. Then she shook her head. "Yes. Actually, no. I have bad news!"

"What happened?" Amber and I asked together.

"It's my dad," Rani said with a sob. "He got a promotion!"

I paused and exchanged glances with Amber. Wasn't a promotion supposed to be a good thing? "You mean . . . he got a better, more important job?" I asked, squinting my eyes.

Rani nodded again.

Amber tilted her head. "Will he be paid more too?"

Rani nodded a third time.

I was definitely missing something. "So . . . what exactly *is* the problem?"

"Well, he didn't say 'yes' yet," Rani said. She started biting her fingernails.

"Why not?"

"Because the job's in London!" Rani blurted out, and she began to cry.

Amber immediately reached out to give her arm a squeeze. June patted Rani on the back. But I was still having trouble understanding.

"That's . . . terrible, Rani," I said. "I know you're going to miss him a lot. How long will he be away?"

"No! Don't you get it?" Rani accepted the packet of tissues June handed to her. "I won't miss him. I'll be *with* him! We'll all have to move!"

I sucked in my breath. "Oooh. *You* won't be missing *him* . . . *we'll* be missing *you.*"

"Right!" Rani groaned. "And I'll miss all of you too!" A fresh batch of tears began to stream down her face.

"When is this supposed to happen?" Amber asked. Her voice was softer and higher than mine. "Like, by this summer?"

"That's the worst part," Rani said with a sniffle. "The job opened up unexpectedly. Dad needs to give them his answer in a week. And if he says 'yes' we'll probably be moving in two weeks!"

Amber and I gasped together.

"But there's more than two *months* left of school!" I shook my head. "It makes no sense to take you out now."

Rani shrugged. "It's supposed to be a really great job."

"No, no," I continued. "We can't let it happen. There's got to be some way to keep you here. I just know it." I patted her on the shoulder. "Don't worry. I'll think of something."

The four of us trudged up to the school, each quietly lost in our own thoughts. June had her head down. Amber was humming something to herself. Rani was still sniffling.

Think of a plan, I commanded myself. I led the pack to the front doors of our building and toward the auditorium where our classes were lining up. It was when we were passing by the main office that it caught my eye. There was a colorful mini-poster on the bulletin board on the wall.

Do you sing? Do you dance? Are you a musician or comedian?
Don't hide your light under a bushel! Sign up for
THE ROLAND LAKE LOWER SCHOOL
Spring Talent Show!